I0652569

William Elliot Griffis, Henry Satoh, Saburo Shimada

Agitated Japan

The Life of Baron Ii Kamon-no-Kami Naosuké

William Elliot Griffis, Henry Satoh, Saburo Shimada

Agitated Japan
The Life of Baron Ii Kamon-no-Kami Naosuké

ISBN/EAN: 9783337166182

Printed in Europe, USA, Canada, Australia, Japan

Cover: Foto ©Raphael Reischuk / pixelio.de

More available books at **www.hansebooks.com**

Portrait of Baron Ii Kamon-no-Kami Naosuké, in his Imperial
court dress, and his autograph poem. (For translation
of the poem see next page).

Ōmi no mi kishi utsu nami no iku tabimo,
Miyo ni kokoro wo kudaki nuru kana.

　　　　Poem by Ii Kamon-no-Kami.

Literal translation : Rocks break the tide and the
Sea of Ōmi is never at rest : So is my soul in its
yearnings for the beloved land.

　　　　Note :—The Sea of Ōmi is the poetical ap-
　　　　pellation of the Lake Biwa. The Baron's
　　　　territory bordered on that lake ; hence,
　　　　the use of its waters for the metaphor.

As beats the ceaseless wave on Ōmi's strand
So breaks my heart for our beloved land.

　　　　　Reviser's Translation.

AGITATED JAPAN

THE

LIFE OF BARON II KAMON-NO-KAMI NAOSUKÉ

(BASED ON THE KAIKOKU SHIMATSU
OF SHIMADA SABURŌ)

BY

H. SATOH
LATE OF THE IMPERIAL COMMERCIAL COLLEGE OF
TOKIO, JAPAN.

REVISED BY
WM. ELLIOT GRIFFIS, D.D.
AUTHOR OF THE MIKADO'S EMPIRE.

TOKIO:
DAI NIPPON TOSHO KABUSHIKI KAISHA:
Z. P. MARUYA & Co.

LONDON:
KEGAN PAUL, TRENCH, TRÜBNER & Co.

NEW YORK:
D. APPLETON & Co.

1896.

PRINTED AT
THE TOKYO-SEISHIBUNSHA.

PREFACE.

Since the appearance of Mr. S. Shimada's book, Kaikoku Shimatsu, (Summary of the Opening of Japan to Civilization), I have been desirous of introducing the great subject of his book more widely to the public of the Land of Liberty, for it was Baron Ii who sacrificed his life in order to conclude a commercial treaty with the United States of America. Having been thus far prevented from accomplishing my purpose, I availed myself of the leisure afforded in a short stay in America, to boldly attempt the writing of an abridged account of the Baron's political and diplomatic career. In so doing I have been encouraged by Dr. W. E. Griffis who kindly undertook to revise my manuscript. Without his help the book would never have been completed.

The facts mentioned are all based on Mr. Shimada's careful investigations embodied in his Kaikoku Shimatsu. I claim no originality except in the arrangement of topics in which I have followed my own judgment, in order to remove difficulties from the minds of readers who are not familiar with the history of Japan. In presenting this little book to the American public, I hope for their kind indulgence. My lack of literary merit is unavoidable, owing to imperfect knowledge of the English language. The style of any passages showing merit is attributable to the scholarly attainments of the reviser, Dr. William Elliot Griffis, the author of "The Mikado's Empire." The commonest things often receive merits through the touch of a master hand. The illustrations have been taken from Kaikoku Shimatsu with the author's permission.

The delay in publishing this book has been

caused by the official duties on which I had to enter immediately on my return from America. The humble service I had to render to the General Headquarters for the Expeditionary Armies during the late hostilities with China required my presence in Hiroshima, and afterwards in Shimonoseki where the Treaty of Peace with China was concluded, and also in Chefoo where the ratifications were exchanged.

H. S.

Tokio, December, 1895.

HISTORY OF THE EMPIRE OF JAPAN

COMPILED AND TRANSLATED

FOR

IMPERIAL JAPANESE COMMISSION

OF THE

WORLD'S COLUMBIAN EXPOSITION
CHICAGO 1893.

———◆———

FOR SALE BY

Z. P. MARUYA & Co.
TOKIO, JAPAN.

CONTENTS.

PREFACE

BY

COL. JOHN A. COCKERILL,

Special Correspondent, " New York Herald."

For nearly fifty years the world has stood in amazement before the wondrous progress, the marvellous achievements of Japan. To the people of the United States this "youngest child of the world's old age" has seemed a veritable protege. To us it was given to draw the blinds which shut this strange, Asiatic race from what we are pleased to term the Higher Civilization. We have been to Japan a friend and admirer. To our schools her youth first appealed. Our friendship has been steadfast; nay, more, we have poured our wealth into her lap in exchange for her incomparable products.

I am pleased to believe that the people of Japan have appreciated our kindly sentiments and that the intelligent men here do not regret the hour that brought our insistent fleet to their gateway.

The history of Japan—the modern Japan—must always be interesting to our people. The men of Japan who had the wisdom and the foresight to maintain the policy of throwing down the barriers which closed their sealocked empire to the world were statesmen who wrought even better than they knew. They merit all honor. To the Baron Ii Kamon-no-Kami, the wise Tairo of the final era of the Tokugara rule, whose deeds are recorded in this work now laid before the English-speaking world by Mr. Satoh—himself a splendid type of the progressive Japanese—both honor and gratitude are due. He changed the destiny of Japan. For years a cloud rested upon his name

because of his new political system—this man
who gave Japan her material prosperity, who
set her on the road to glory and whose life was
sacrificed that his country might take its place
in the sisterhood of nations. Like Cromwell
and Washington and scores of masterful leaders
who have advanced peoples into the sunlight
of progress and intelligence, Baron Ii Naosuké's
name has passed from obloquy to universal
reverence. Modern Japan reveres and honors
his name and his work. The people of our
great Republic, who are indebted to him for
the crowning success of the Perry Expedition,
our first commercial treaty, will delight to
know of him and will be proud to honor his
memory.

It is with pleasure that I commend to my
countrymen—the great majority of whom I
believe share with me my admiration for
the striving, earnest-purposed, ever-ambitious

people of Japan—this timely biography of
one of Japan's most potential and valuable
servitors.

JOHN A. COCKERILL.

Miyanoshita, Japan.

December 21st 1895.

————————

PREFACE

BY

CAPT. F. BRINKLEY R. A.

If western students of Japanese history could obtain a clear insight into the development of public opinion in Japan during the years preceding the Restoration, they would be able to resolve a riddle that has long perplexed them. Changes so radical as those that Japan has undergone during the past thirty years, must necessarily be suspected of superficiality, and therefore of impermanence, unless it can be shown that they were prefaced by an appropriate growth of national sentiment. But apparently there is nothing either shallow or transient in these changes, and the inference is

then forced upon us that they came when the
country was ripe for them. How was that
condition of ripeness brought about? What
influence had been working silently before the
Meiji era to undermine feudalism and prepare
the minds of the people for the reception of so
many phases of Western civilization? These
questions, vital to any intelligent perception of
the Japanese problem, can be answered only by
profound and minute study of the social, indus-
trial, and political story of the Tokugawa
Epoch. Such a study is practically beyond the
reach of foreigners, owing to the almost in-
superable difficulties that they encounter in
obtaining access to sources of information. It
must be undertaken by Japanese historians,
and even of these very few can be expected to
possess the necessary qualifications. Prominent among the few must be placed Mr. Shimada Saburo, one of Japan's leading politicians

and thinkers, who now supplements his numerous contributions to Japanese literature by an
able sketch of the life of the great feudal
chieftain and far-seeing statesman, Ii Kamon-
no-kami, perhaps the most conspicuous figure
in the drama of the Restoration. The memoir
deserves careful perusal, not only for the sake
of the light that it throws on Japan's passage
from the old to the new, but also because it
helps to enforce the truth that, if some sangui-
nary and cruel acts were committed against
foreign life in the years immediately preceding
the Meiji era, they had their origin not so much
in the hearts of the people as in the political
turmoil of the time. Perhaps this latter lesson
does not any longer need to be inculcated.
Perhaps those that profess to find traces of
anti-foreign bias still lurking beneath Japanese
urbanity and liberalism, see in reality a reflec-
tion of their own racial prejudice rather than a

true image of Japanese feeling. However that may be, these interesting pages of history, compiled by Mr. Shimada and excellently translated by Mr. H. Satoh, will help in some measure to dispel a delusion that certainly tends to hold Japanese and foreigners asunder.

F. Brinkley.

Tokyo, January 5th., 1896.

REVISER'S INTRODUCTION.

When in June, 1890, with the aid of a
Japanese friend, Rev. T. Harada, of Tōkiō,
I read the book here condensed in English, I
said at once, "This is the typical new book in
New Japan." In The Literary World of May
6, 1893, I have described the work and indicated
its relations to the literary movement in Japan.
On hearing from Mr. Satoh of his proposed
translation, I encouraged him to proceed. My
work of revision,—a labor of love, as an American who honors the memory of the noble
dead,—has been in some slight corrections of
idiom and the consecution of tenses, with dates
in the Gregorian style, and a few notes. I am
glad to add a leaf to the wreath laid on an
honored tomb.

The title, Kaikoku Shimatsu, means literally,

"Opening of the Country, Beginning and End."
The author is Mr. Shimada Saburō, editor of a
widely circulating daily newspaper at Tōkiō.
He is a scholar in English, a traveller in Europe
and America, and a member of the Liberal
Party, holding a seat as representative in the
Lower House of the Imperial Diet. He is
still in the early forties, and educationally is
one of the fruits of American missionary enter-
prise. His work marks a new era in Japanese
historiography. Even the searching criticisms
of those whose sympathies, from memory and
loyalty, are with the old House of Mito have not
been able to invalidate his statements. One
can easily see that Mr. Shimada has trained
himself to write history according to the canons
of the science in vogue in Christendom.

The reviser's first sight of Japanese humanity
was in Philadelphia in 1860, when the first
embassy ever sent from Japan to the United

States proceeded up Walnut Street in carriages. What impressed the boy-spectator even more than their magnificent garments and their superb swords, was the elegant culture, the easy politeness of these hermit-islanders from that East which was so far as to be on our West. It was while in America that these oriental gentlemen heard of the cruel death of their master. This was in reality the first blood shed in what was to be a prolonged civil war, lasting fitfully from 1860 to 1870. The Orient and the Occident had come into collision and the struggle is still going on, nor is the end yet. After Japan's must come China's turn to reform.

Later on, when out of college and in Japan, laying some of the first foundation stones of the national system of free public education, I made myself not only acquainted but familiar with the men and scenes described in this book.

The white walls of the castle of Hikoné, and the
streets of the lake-town, and in Yedo the mansion, route of visit to the Shōgun's palace, the
scenes of the assassination, the Sakurada Gate
and the interior of the grounds first Shōgunal
and then Imperial, are all clear pictures in my
mind's eye. Still further, with nearly all of the
survivors mentioned in this book, and some of
those now passed away, I enjoyed personal
acquaintance and, with several, familiar
friendship.

One of the mightiest problems before the
whole world and to all humanity is the recon-
ciliation of the oriental and the occidental
civilizations. Such a task is worthy of the
noblest powers of the statesman, philosopher,
and seeker after God. In the roll of those who
have achieved success in this difficult and
delicate work, Williams, Perry, Harris, Parkes,
Iwakura, and others, that of Ii Kamon no Kami

stands not least. Despite the limitations of his age and nationality, he achieved a noble work. He fell a martyr to truth. For a generation his memory has suffered, as most men temporarily unsuccessful but ultimately vindicated usually suffer. The foreign as well as the native books of the seventh, eighth, and ninth decades of this century are full of his "swaggering" and "bullying" spirit, and nothing was too vile to say about the murdered Premier.

Yet as Cromwell had his Carlyle, so has Ii had his Shimada. Cleansed from insult and stain, we now behold a sincere patriot, possessing indeed the human infirmities common to mortals in Old Japan, but who read the signs of the times and saved his country from India's fate and China's humiliation. Drawing back the bolts from the inside, Ii opend Japan to the civilization of Christendom. He saved his country from bloodshed by aliens, probably also from conquest and dismemberment, by shedding his own. Americans who wish to see Asia civilized and Christianized,—but not in the British way of conquest as in the case of India, or of opium-forcing and land-seizure as in the case of China, and who even expect mutual blessings to come from mutual benevolence, as the West receives benefits from the East, will welcome this narrative. It tells the story from the inside of agitated Japan. It complements handsomely the numerous European and American narratives of travel and diplomacy in Japan, written during the early part of this generation. Incidentally, the work sheds lustre upon the whole work of Townsend Harris, the unmarried and solitary first American Minister Resident in Japan.

Wm. Elliot Griffis.

Ithaca N.Y. March 20 1894.

PREFACE TO KAIKOKU SHIMATSU
BY VISCOUNT ŌKUBO ICHI-Ō.

(Translation.)

A perusal of Kaikoku Shimatsu reminds me
of the old days. On the evening of the 24th
day of the 6th month of the 5th year of Anséi
era (1858), when I went to see the Tairō, Baron
Ii, to inform him of my departure to Kiōto on
the following day, I told him that as to the
appointment of the Shōgun's heir, I had heard
it directly from the Shōgun himself; but as to
the question of foreign affairs, I said that I had
embodied my opinion in a poem, and asked him
if that were his view. I had the poem written
on my pocket paper and presented it to his consideration. He carefully perused it and said
that he approved of it, instructing me at the
same time to act up to the spirit of that poem.

Now, I have the pleasure of appending that poem here as an evidence that the Baron was in favor of opening the country to intercourse with foreign nations. The poem reads :—

"However numerous, and diversified the nations of the earth may be, the God who reigns over them all (or, binds them together) can never be more than one."

(Signed) Ōkubo Ichi-ō.

N. B. Viscount Ōkubo held an important position under the Tokugawa Shōgunate. His departure to Kiōto, referred to in his preface, was in reference to his official errand to the Imperial Court. When the new system of peerage was established by the reigning Emperor, he was made a viscount in recognition of his political services before and after the Restoration. At the time of writing Kaikoku Shimatsu he was still living and was looked up to as one of the living authorities of the history of those days when Baron Ii was at the head of the government.

PREFACE TO KAIKOKU SHIMATSU BY PROF. NAKAMURA MASANAO.[*]

———

The power of sincerity may call up the
departed spirit, and open communication with
the other world. Observing the existence of
party feelings, and the frequency of partial
representation of facts on the pages of historical writings, it has awakened in the
breast of my friend, Mr. Shimada, a strong
desire to correct those misrepresentations. As
the fruit of his sincerity, he has succeeded in
freeing Baron Ii from the undeserving dishonor
in which he had been buried. This work of
Mr. Shimada had its origin in the 27th anniversary of the Baron's death,—which cannot
be looked upon as a mere accident. It is

———

* The original is in Classic Chinese.

wonderful, when we consider that the departed
spirit apparently chose a person to whom to
entrust the custody of his private papers and
through him to deliver them to Mr. Shimada.
The power of sincerity is sure to find an echo.
Who can say that consciousness has no place in
the departed spirit ?

(Signed) Kei-u Nakamura Masanao.

N. B. Professor Nakamura was one of the professors
of Chinese literature in the University of Tokugawa
Shōgunate. He studied English when every body
was opposed to it. His widened view, by his study of
that literature, placed him above his colleagues, and
with the opening of the new period of Japan's history,
his name became synonymous with erudition. He
was looked upon as one of the few literary geniuses
of that era. He had a school of his own from which
many able men were sent out to the world. He died
a few years ago and was lamented by all, high and
low, cultured and illiterate. Among his many books,
translated in Japanese, Mill on Liberty, The Constitu-

tion of the United States, English Literature etc., his translation of Smile's Self-help was almost universally read by the literary circle of Japan, and is now held in high esteem.

POEM TO KAIKOKU SHIMATSU BY COUNT KATSU.

(Translation.)

The proud pine though evergreen, and with outspread branches in the balmy air of the Land of the Rising Sun, may suffer decay in its roots buried deep in the heart of the earth; or, a worm eating into its substantial stem, it may fall before the tempest, or break under the heaping snow.

Ah, thou who didst brave the storm which came raging from over the great sea, who didst make a shelter before the heaping snow of dangers and difficulties, who didst thus sacrifice thy life for thy country, how hast thou fallen a miserable victim to the frailties of the world! Yet true to the dying instruction of him whom thou hast served, thou didst set little store on thine own weal. Neither before rank nor power didst thou falter. Straight in the course of law, thou didst never deviate.

Richly dost thou deserve to be ranked with the few worthies that adorn the House of the Ruler over this land. Yet not only was this honor refused thee, but thy merit was the cause of thy death. On the evergreen pine, now dead and fallen, has malice heaped shame and dishonor, with none to plead on its behalf!

But time flies and passes away, its good and its evil, all vanish like a dream. Now in this reign of Sacred Wisdom, thy hidden merits began to appear, embodied in this book. The fallen pine has regained its life. Its new foliage will thrive in this reign of wisdom. Let the blessings of the Great Sovereign be remembered with gratitude, and be impressed deep on heart and memory, as long as mind and memory last.

(Signed) Kaishin Katsu Awa.*

Late Autumn,

20th year of Meiji (1887).

---

* Ex-Minister of Navy under the Shōgun and Mikado. He commanded the first Japanese steamship which crossed the Pacific Ocean and brought out the embassy from Yedo to the United States in 1859. Still living.

PREFACE* TO KAIKOKU SHIMATSU BY FIELD MARSHAL COUNT YAMA-GATA† EX-MINISTER-PRESIDENT OF STATE.

(Translation.)

During the time of the Tokugawa Shōgunate,
Japan's intercourse with foreign nations was
limited to China and Holland. Hence the
people knew little of the civilization of other
nations. Peace universally reigned. The
swords were kept in their sheaths and the
arrows were enclosed in their quivers. Luxury
and effeminacy followed in the wake of peace.
The sudden appearance of the problem of
foreign intercourse in the 6th year of the era of
Kayéi (1853) resulted in the universal cry of

---

* The original is in Classic Chinese.

† Called by the Western press the Moltke of the
East.

exclusion. The power of the Shōgunate was gradually undermined by this new event.

It is not to be wondered at that this cry was raised on every side, for people were kept in utter ignorance of things outside of their country. Their condition was like that of a frog in a well.* Things outside were completely shut up from their view. Along with this perplexity, the advocates of the virtual authority of the Throne, assailed the Tokugawa Shōgunate. Baron Ii was the person who had to face these great problems. Confident in the wisdom of his policy, he bravely opposed public opinion, and was hated even by his relations. The result was that he had to sacrifice his life for the policy he followed.

Yet this sad event not only saved our country from the misfortune that befell our neighbor,

---

* The frog in the well knows not the great ocean—
Japanese proverb. G.

China, but opened the pathway of civilization in our own land. This merit is attributable to no one but Baron Ii.

Mr. Shimada has prepared a biography of the Baron, under the title of Kaikoku Shimatsu. (Summary of the Opening of the Country.) On perusal I find that his representation is both powerful and impartial. His penetrating insight is coupled with his literary power. In Mr. Shimada's ability, mental and literary, Baron Ii has found an able advocate that has lifted him up out of the malice and enmity in which he had been so long buried.

(Signed) Count* Yamagata Aritomo.

11th month, 20th year of Meiji.

(November 20, 1887.)

---

* Now Marquis. Promoted to that rank in recognition of his noble and successful service as Commander-in-chief of the First Expeditionary Army during the Japano-Chinese war.

His Imperial Highness Prince Kita-
shirakawa honored Mr. Shimada's Kaikoku Shimatsu, with his autograph of
four Chinese characters meaning:

" Heaven's ordination baffles the
human."

Signed Kiodo, (the nom-de-plume
of the Prince).

———————

INTRODUCTORY CHAPTER.

Without the least taint of flattery it may be safely asserted that Japan is indebted to no other country so much as to the United States. This indebtedness began on her first trial of that international intercourse which she has kept up ever since, and will doubtlessly continue as long as the world shall last. It is an undeniable fact that the honor of having opened the hitherto secluded Empire of Japan to foreign intercourse, commercial and otherwise, rests with the United States. Although in the order of chronology, the priority of commercial relations with Japan belongs to the Netherlands, yet the actual opening of the Empire

to active foreign intercourse dates from the
time when Commodore M. C. Perry was
sent by the American government to knock
at the door which had been kept closed for
hundreds of years.

The sudden appearance of the American
war-ships off Uraga in 1853 acted on Japan
like the sounds of a cannonade in the ears
of a warrior who, after years of hard fighting had been slumbering in perfect enjoyment of undisturbed rest. "Be up and
doing" was echoed and re-echoed throughout the length and breadth of the whole
Empire. Not to speak of the mass of
people, even the so-called educated class
knew little of the serious consequence
involved in their actions. The cry "repel
the foreigner" was heard on every side.
This party of exclusion quickly found

adherents in every part of the Empire.
The castle of Yedo in which the " Tycoon"
or Shōgun had his seat of government was
assailed on every side with the demand for
obedience to the traditions of seclusion.
The Shōgunate found itself between the
dilemma of foreign intercourse and civil
war. The Rōju, or Senators of the Shōgunate, were divided amongst themselves,
and the results of this division were seen
in frequent changes in the personnel of
this Senate or Cabinet of the Tokugawa
Government which had ruled in Yedo
since A.D. 1603.

Request of time for consideration had
been made to the American envoy, Perry,
on his first coming to Japan, but now the
matter could not be put off under the same
excuse. The question had to be referred

to the Emperor in Kiōto, but no favorable
answer was received. The Daimiō, or
Barons of the land had been consulted, but
they were in favor of isolation. The officers
of the Shōgunate knew well the impossibility of refusing intercourse with foreign
nations. Placed between two conflicting
elements, the Tokugawa government in
Yedo could make no advance in either way.
Yet the thing could not be left in abeyance
any longer. Sufficient time for consideration had been granted by the American
envoy and the answer must be given.

Among the Princes of Tokugawa lineage,
Prince Rekko of Mito, better known in
annals of those days as the Senior Prince
of Mito, was the most powerful and zealous
advocate of the exclusion policy. Even if
there had been a single daimiō who knew

the impossibility of keeping the country
closed, public opinion was such, and the
power of the Exclusion Party was so
great, that he dared not express his own
convictions. Since the establishment of
the Tokugawa family nothing had shaken
the whole empire like this question of
foreign intercourse.

Hitherto it had been the policy of the
Shōgun to decide political matters without
reference either to the Imperial Court or
to the daimiōs. In a word, his govern-
ing power was unlimited; and this was
never disputed by the Emperor or his
Court. When in the seventeenth century,
the order to close the country to foreign
commerce had been issued, Iyeyasu
never referred the question, great as it
was, to the Emperor for his approval, nor

did the Imperial Cabinet ever blame him
for so doing.   In other words, the Shōgun
was invested with nearly absolute rule.
Having once possessed the power to close
the whole country to foreign commerce,
and to prohibit Japanese subjects from
going abroad, why should the Yedo government hesitate now in making decisive
answer to the American demands?   Why
did it not enter into a commercial treaty
with the United States, if it deemed it to
be of any interest to the nation?   Why
was it that, instead of taking the whole
responsibility on itself, it referred the
question to the Mikado and to the daimiōs?

In explanation of this apparent deviation
from the policy hitherto followed two
things offer themselves :

(1)   The Cabinet of the Shōgun lacked

an able leader bold enough to take the whole responsibility on his own shoulders.

(2) The officers of the Shōgunate were sufficiently acquainted with the spirit of the times outside of Japan, which clearly showed them the difficulty of strictly adhering to the traditions of exclusion, and yet they feared the public opinion at home.

The Tokugawas had, up to this time, enjoyed an undisputed rule over the whole land for more than two hundred years ; yet it seems there could be no exception to the inevitable tendency to weakness and degeneracy which attends upon long enjoyment of peaceful rule. History is full of similar instances.

The Tokugawas after the eighth Shōgun (Yoshimuné, 1717–1744) began to show signs of effeminacy and decay. The hardy

race of soldiers who had hitherto guarded
the honor and power of the House founded
by Iyéyasu sought enjoyment, not in the
exercise of arms, but in music and dancing.
This tendency culminated at the time of the
thirteenth of the line, Iyésada, (1833-1858)
generally called Onkiō-in. His period of
rule, though of short duration was unlike
any of his predecessors in outward refine-
ment and enjoyment of ease. Factors
were already at work which were under-
mining the power of the Tokugawas.
These, though they did not come to the
surface, were actively operative, concealed
under guise of fidelity to the Shōgunate
and quiet submission to its rule. Let but
an occasion arise and those factors were
ready to start up in opposition to the Yedo
autocrat.

Divided within, and critically watched without, the Shōgunate suddenly found itself confronted with the insoluble problem of foreign intercourse. The whole country was at once left in anxious suspense. Only extraordinary ability and rare foresight could effect complete deliverance. Never was the need of an able pilot so keenly felt as at this time of opposing currents which involved the whole country in a state of ceaseless commotion. The only way to obtain a man for the hour lay in the abolition of the long established custom of limiting eligibility to the Shōgunate by lineal or political influence. The gateway to responsible position in the government must be thrown wide open so as to admit men of desired abilities. Hence it was that at this time the instances of promotion were more frequent, while abnormally rapid, than at any time, since the establishment of the Yedo government by the great, if not the greatest statesman of the land of Yamato—Prince Tokugawa Iyéyasu.

Wisdom and ability were naturally sought among the students of the Yedo University (Shōhéiko) and many were selected therefrom to fill important posts. But the long established methods of choosing officers could not at once undergo so great a renovation as to admit any of those students to the high office of Rōju or Senator. However able and qualified the graduates of the University might be, they never rose higher than to the offices of Métsuké* (Overseer) and Bugiō, Governor

---

* The O-métsuké or "spy" of European books on Japan. G.

or Director). As such, however, they were
no doubt consulted by the Senators on
matters of great importance. The office of
Rōjū was only open to those Daimiō or
Barons who submitted themselves as vas-
sals to Prince Iyéyasu before he became
the Shōgun or Mikado's lieutenant. This
class in the landed nobility was called the
Retainer Barons (Fudai Daimiō) in con-
tradistinction to those Daimiō who had
been Lords of provinces (Koku-shu) before
the Tokugawa Shōgunate was established.
When these Province-lords yielded to the
authority of the Yedo government, they
were suffered to hold their inherited lands
under the obligation of submitting themselves to the rule of the Tokugawas acting
as lieutenants of the Emperor, or Shōguns.

It was out of the Fudai or Retainer

Barons that the high officers were appointed. The official positions next in grade, such as overseers, directors, etc., were filled by Hatamoto, or Supporters of the Flag, one of the military classes that formed the personal guard of the Shōgun.

According to the constitution of the Yedo government, it was possible to appoint an officer who should rank above the Rōju or Senators. Tairō was the name of that highest office. Literally it means the Great Elder, and may be translated President-Senator. A Tairō was to be appointed in times of great urgency only, and on no other occasions. But sometimes this title was given to some one in recognition of his meritorious services. The authority vested in the Tairō was dictatorial. Nobody, except the Shōgun, had a

right to say aught against what he commanded. There were not many in the
whole history of the Tokugawas (1603–
1868) who were appointed to this highest
office, and the subject of this brief biography
was the last Tairō. To foreigners he was
usually known as the Go-Tairō. The first
syllable being purely honorary.

The times were such, as we have already
mentioned, that without an able guiding
hand, the whole country might easily be
involved in irreparable strife, commotion,
and woe. Without a bold statesman who
could bear the whole responsibility on his
own shoulders. without a sincere patriot
prepared to die for the cause of his country,
and without diplomatic talent backed by
keen insight into the future of Japan, the
whole empire might fall a miserable prey

to the dangerous strifes of political factions
and party rivalries. Thanks be to Heaven,
this great ability and a patriotism sufficient
to meet the requirement of the times were
found in the person of the Lord of Hikone
Castle, Baron Ii Naosuke by name, better
known in foreign annals as Ii Kamon-no-
Kami.

Yet this man's merits, varied and extraordinary as they were, had as yet
scarcely commanded public recognition. A
majority of the politicians and public
writers of those days, were either ignorant
of current thought outside of Japan, or
were so blinded by their political prejudices,
that they not only failed to appreciate the
rare merits of the great Baron, but they
openly attacked his policy and loudly
cried : " Exclusion ! Exclusion ! No foreign

barbarians in this land of gods."

Even if there were some who approved
of his policy, and clearly saw the necessity
of opening intercourse with foreign nations,
the power of the Exclusion Party was so
predominant that they dared not express
their own ideas. If there were a few
brave enough to publish their approbation
of Baron Ii's policy, their voices were soon
drowned by the almost universal cries of
exclusion and isolation. The political
opponents of the great Baron would not
have hesitated to call him publicly a rebel,
or a betrayer of national interest, if they
were only free to express their feelings.
In private conversation and correspond-
ence, they applied to him every name that
malice and hatred could invent.

The great man was so much in advance

of his times, that what he did for his country was not appreciated until many years after his death. His foresight was so far-reaching that in what his contemporaries saw nothing but unmixed evil, he clearly beheld benefit and advantage for the future of his beloved country. While he lived, and for many years after his cruel assassination, his name was remembered only as that of a selfish autocrat. Making a determined stand against public opinion, he could not help but create bitter political enemies, while his arguments so much in advance of his times, and his strict adherence to the interest of the Tokugawa Shōgunate, made not a few personal enemies, both among the officers of the government and the Princes and Barons of the land. His cruel assassination was nothing else than an outcome of bitter feelings against him, political as well as personal in their nature.

According to feudal law, if any one in the military classes, gentry or Barons, were assassinated, the pension and land entailed upon the person assassinated, were liable to confiscation, and the family to be politically extinguished.

Baron Ii Naosuké was assassinated. Should his baronetcy be confiscated and his title be extinguished? Should the most prominent among the Retainer Barons be cast out of the great honor and privilege? Should he who died a martyr to the interest of the whole Empire be deprived of the rank of a Baron? The assassins except one, were those who had been retainers of the Prince of Mito, who was the greatest political opponent of the dead statesman. Naturally enough, the retainers of the unfortunate Baron understood the cruel act as originating from the Clan of Mito. Revenge on Mito was the only thought among the followers of the Lord of Hikoné, and attempts at vengeance would have involved the two powerful clans in bloody strife. Let war be once declared, and the consequence would have been far more serious than at other times.

One party in the Hikoné Clan worked hard to escape, if possible, the penalty attending the unfortunate death of the beloved master. In order at least to lessen the impending penalty, the two confidential secretaries of the great Baron, Nagano Shuzen and Utsugi Rokunojo, were put to death. The spirit of revenge

grew more and more among the Hikoné
Clan, but with great difficulty it was
pacified. This was done by calling the
attention of the excited men to the instruction that had been given by one of their
former lords, Naotaka by name, which
happily served to stifle for a while all serious agitation. Implicit obedience to the
Tokugawa government was clearly set forth
in this instruction, which, having been
issued by him who was counted among the
greatest of the Lords of Hikoné, exerted a
sufficiently potent influence to pacify the
excitement agitating the whole clan.

Here again the already disturbed Shōgunate found itself face to face with another
great problem—the confiscation of territory
and extinction of the title of first in rank
among the Retainer Barons; but for-

tunately it did not abide by the letter of the
law.   The Yedo government satisfied legal
requirements by confiscating only a part of
the baronial land.

The great, and to some, the terrible
Tairō being dead, attacks on the Shōgun's
policy became louder and louder.   Along
with these assaults the name of Ii Kamon-
no-Kami came to be ranked with those of
*chō-teki,** traitors or rebels.   The feeling
against him was so bitter that in order to
prevent any further misfortune falling upon
the Clan of Hikoné, it became necessary to
burn up all the official papers and records
of him who was now classed, by the in-
flamed public opinion of the times, among
the worst of rebels and enemies of the land.

* For the awful associations of this word, in
Japanese history, see The Mikado's Empire, index.

It was given out that those documents had been committed to fire by two of the Baron's retainers, Rinhoji and Ōkubo.

Nevertheless Ōkubo managed to save the precious documents. " There will be nothing," he said, " to prove the sincerity and unmixed fidelity of Lord Naosuké, if these papers be destroyed. Whatever may come, I dare not burn them. If my secret concealment of these papers be exposed, then will I burn them, and atone for the guilt of concealment by killing myself. I am determined to preserve these precious documents at the risk of my life."

These words were spoken to Rinhoji when he advised Ōkubo of the danger of keeping the valuable papers, but when on every side they were believed to have been consumed to ashes, they came forth to serve a noble purpose. They save the home of a great statesman and patriot from the shame and dishonor in which it had long been buried.

The able instrument of this noble service is Mr. Shimada Saburō. The occasion was the 19th year of Meiji, 1886. Then, Ōkubo, who had survived his friend, Riuhoji, felt safe for the first time since their concealment, in bringing out those valuable papers before those who assembled at the sepulchre of Riuhoji to celebrate the anniversary of his death. It was entirely through the deceased man's secrecy that Ōkubo had been enabled to save those papers as well as his own life. Mr. Shimada Saburō had already been seeking materials for the biography of Baron Ii

Naosuké, but such data as he could obtain
were far from impartial and satisfactory.
At last he heard of the existence of the
original papers These were gladly lent
him, and from them, and from what he
could gather from living authorities, he
succeeded in compiling a book which is
now ranked among the great works of the
Méiji era. The appearance of his book
was like a new star in the literary sky of
new Japan.

Before committing to print, copies of
the book were distributed among those
persons for criticism, who were acquainted
with the politics and public opinion of the
days before 1861. The book was then
published with those criticisms in a form
of notes. This fact, together with a careful
study on the part of the author, makes the

work doubly valuable and authentic as a
historical record.   The criticisms are very
favorable, and at the same time confirm
the conclusion which the author draws
from his own studies and observations.

Besides his disinterested loyalty to the
Tokugawa Shōgunate the great merit of
Baron Ii Kamon-no-Kami as a remarkable
statesman and an able diplomat, lies in his
conclusion of a commercial treaty with the
United States.

To his compatriots, Mr. Shimada has
shown, through his book, the admirable
merits of this great man, but no biography
of him has yet been written in English, so
that his true merits have not been fully
made known to the American public.   The
artist Shima Sekka who was a sincere
admirer of the Baron, carved his statue in

wood and exhibited the work at the World's
Columbian Exposition in Chicago. It was
then presented by the sculptor to the
Museum of Washington, D. C., where it
now stands as a memorial of him who
sacrificed his life to secure the friendly relations now existing between the United
States and the Empire of Japan.

" Nothing is worse than a barrier against the communication of thought."

Naosuké.

CHAPTER I.

Naosuké was the fourteenth son of Baron Ii Kamon-no-kami Naonaka. He was born on the 29th day of the tenth month of the twelfth year of Bunkwa era (November 30, A.D. 1815). The family of Ii is a very old one. Its record goes as far back as the latter part of tenth century. Its ancestor Bitchiu Tarō rendered meritorious service to the Emperor Ichijō (A. D. 987-1011) in subduing the rebels of Yezo.* He was rewarded with the ownership of the place in which he was born, viz., Iidani (Valley

---

* Yezo was the northern part of the empire occupied by the barbarians or uncivilized Ainos.

of Ii) in the Province of Tōtōmi, where
he built his castle in which his des-
cendants continued to live until the
time of Naomasa. The family name of Ii
was taken from that of the place where
the castle stood.

It was Naomasa who first formed an
intimate connection with Prince Iyéyasu,
the founder of the Tokugawa Shōgunate
under which Japan was restored after long
civil wars to a universal peace which lasted
for nearly three hundred years. In recognition of the faithful service rendered by
Naomasa in the great work of bringing the
whole land under the rule of the Shōgunate,
the first Tokugawa Shōgun, Iyéyasu, made
him Lord of the Castle of Hikoné, with
greatly increased territory. He also gave
him the foremost rank among the Fudai

or Retainer Barons.   To him and his
family belonged the honor of protectorship
of the Imperial City of Kiôto and for this
reason the family of Ii was stationed in
Hikoné, which is within a short distance
of the Imperial city.*

The father of the subject of this biography was the thirteenth Lord from Naomasa.
According to the usage of the Ii family,
all the sons except the eldest who was the
heir, were either given as adopted sons to
other Barons, or were converted into retainers with a pension which was generally
very small.   The law of progeniture, the
exceptions being in cases of insanity or
bodily defect only, was enforced throughout
the Empire.   Naosuké being the fourteenth

* The Mikado's Empire, 276.

in order, there was little or no hope of his
accession to the Lordship of the Hikoné
Clan.   His   elder   brothers,   except   the
eldest, had been adopted into other families
and had thus become the lords of their
respective clans.   Naosuké still lived in his
father's territory.   The pecuniary allow-
ance he received from the family was so
small that he must needs lead a quiet life,
no better than that of an ordinary samurai.
He had a small house built for himself,
where he spent the whole of his time in
military exercises and literary pursuits.
All of his friends were of gentle, but not
lordly birth.   Among   these he found
Nagano Shuzen, who afterward became
one of the two confidential assistants who
helped him to steer through the boisterous
seas of political factions.

Naosuké was seventeen years of age
when he moved into his private residence.
Four years afterward, he had to go to Yedo
(the present Tōkiō) where the Baron of
Hikoné had his regular mansion within
the enclosure of Yedo Castle, in a locality
known as Sakurada or Cherry-field.   According to the law of the Shōgunate, the
Daimiō, besides the castles in their respective provinces, were required to have one
or more mansions in Yedo. They were
obliged to live every alternate year in one
of the two places.

Naosuké's journey to Yedo in this case
was not to meet the requirement of this
law for he was as yet only a private man.
In the following year, he came back to
Hikoné, where his time was spent in
attending the academy of the clan or School

of Chinese Learning which had been established by the Lord of the Castle for the
military and literary education of the
retainers.

By nature, Naosuké was a man of a
remarkably strong will and firm decision.
He was earnest and serious in anything he
attempted. Whatever he did, his whole
soul was in it. His qualifications for
statesmanship in times of turbulance were
already visible in his youth. " A military
man," he used to say, " must always be
prepared for emergencies," and this principle showed itself in his daily conduct.
Once decided, he was as firm as a rock.
No amount of difficulties would make him
falter or find him irresolute. What he had
aimed at he would persevere in till he
would win. His obscure private life, dur-

Private Residence

Iōsuké in Hikoné.

ing which he could observe every grade of human life, was a fit preparation for the great career reserved for him.   In those days it was a rare opportunity for a Baron's son to study the ways and thoughts of ordinary people, and at the same time to exercise his ability in contending against varied difficulties unknown to persons of higher birth.

Naosuké afterward came and lived in Yedo, where in 1850 he heard of the serious illness of his brother, the Baron.   He immediately obtained from the Yedo government a permit to leave for Hikoné.   As it was against the usage of the times for any Baron to make a journey at so short a notice, his aged retainers at Hikoné remonstrated against his departure from the usual custom.   "What is usage," said he

in one of his letters, "if an opportunity be
lost thereby ?   Before it shall be too late.
I am determined to go."   An express
message again reached him in Yedo, and
he immediately started for his province.
Before he reached his destination, however,
a report of the Baron's death was received,
and he, instead of pursuing his journey,
turned back and came to Yedo.

Naosuké's eldest brother who had succeeded to his father's estate, had no male
issue, and Naosuké, now twenty-seven years
old, was appointed the heir-apparent of the
Hikoné Baronetcy. This was an occurrence quite unexpected, that the fourteenth
son of the late Baron, leading a common
quiet life in a corner of a town on lake
Biwa should be raised to the heirship of
t e great Baronetcy.   But here it was

that a way was opened for the full play
of that rare ability and that strong will
which were combined in the future Baron
of Hikoné.   Thus it was that a passage
was cut for a guiding spirit which the
tendency of the times needed so much.
This important event of his life was
in 1846.

CHAPTER II.

Naosuké as Baron of Hikoné.

On the 21st day of the 11th month of the same year, (Christmas day, 1850), Naosuké was publicly authorized by the Shōgunate to succeed to the Baronetcy and Baronage of Hikoné and to assume the title of Kamon-no-Kami.

Here it is worth while to notice that, at a time when so much importance was attached to the traditional usage, Naosuké's sudden departure against the remonstrances of aged followers, and also against common custom, was no slight presage of that strength of will and keenness of foresight which afterward showed themselves in his

political and diplomatic career. In an age
of dangerous conservatism, these two
qualities placed him beyond the clutch of
the so-called customs and traditions. He
rose superior to these and at the sacrifice
of his life, opened for his country a way of
progress and development hitherto unat-
tained.

Because of the firm stand he made
against his political opponents, Naosuké
has been represented as too obstinate and
proud to receive advice. On the contrary,
a letter which he personally wrote, in
response to a representation made by one
of his retainers, fully shows that he not
only kept the gate wide open to any sincere
advisers but also encouraged them to tender
suggestions freely. The amount of confidence he placed in his two secretaries also

fully indicates his capacity to avail himself
of the views of others. When once he
saw his way, he was immoveable as a rock,
but until then his mind was quite open to
counsels and monitions from whatever
source they might come. Again in instructions which he gave to his clansmen upon
his accession to the Baronetcy, there is a
clause which especially sets forth the necessity of communicating popular feelings
to one's Lord. He encouraged his retainers, irrespective of their class, office, or
condition, to be ready to open their mind
on anything of political or social importance. " Nothing," he said, " is worse than
a barrier against the communication of
thought. Let any and all of you be free
and outspoken on matters of importance."

His succession to the Baronetcy was also

marked by a liberal donation of 15,000 Riō (dollars) to his clansmen. This was no small sum in those days when money was much dearer than at present. This was the surplus amount realized during his brother's administration, and he attributed this gift not to himself, but to his deceased brother. " This gift is from my predecessor," he wrote. " He came to an untimely end before he could carry out his desire to distribute the sum among his retainers."

Naosuké also introduced several reforms in the government of his clan, among which the most conspicuous was the cancellation of an instruction by which the retainers were required to have their family treasures stored up in the public storehouses of the clan. They were dissatisfied, though silent about this and were eager to see a change; when to their joy those treasures were returned to their respective owners. He also made several trips through his territory so as to observe the actual state of affairs.

A case was once brought up before him for decision, which had stood for years unsettled. It was a dispute of a boundary line between two villages. Each party had its own reason to advance, and the case was looked up to as one of the most difficult to decide. The new Baron went to the place in dispute and finding there were natural barriers between the two villages, he gave a clear decision that those lines which nature had drawn should be the boundary from that time and forever. Owing to the complicated nature of the

case, the former judges had been more or
less influenced by the arguments advanced
by one of the parties who would not have
the natural barrier recognized as the
boundary line. This cause of much trouble
and great expense to the contesting parties
during a long period was now so clearly
removed that it left no seed of doubt or
dispute.

Naosuke also encouraged the military
and literary education of his clansmen.
Those proficient in either of the two branches did not escape his notice and patron-
age. The learning and experience of Nakagawa Rokurō was highly esteemed by the
new Baron. It was this man who showed
the impossibility of the further exclusion
of Japan from foreign intercourse. It was
he who influenced the future Tairō to

make a bold departure from the old traditions. It was through his careful investigations of the affairs both at home and
abroad that Naosuké was led to make a
firm stand against the public opinion of his
time. Yet this advanced view of Nakagawa
involved him in shame, and his name,
together with that of his master and of the
Baron's two secretaries, was classed by the
Exclusion Party with the enemies of
Japan's national interests. These four
men were looked down upon as betrayers
of the long-sustained dignity and sacredness of the Land of the Rising Sun.

When in 1853 the question of foreign
intercourse was referred to the Barons of
the land, most of them were in favor of
exclusion, while some of them expressed
the inadvisability of seclusion at the expense

of peace. But none of them proposed a
scheme whereby the interest of the nation
could be upheld. Naosuke's answer to
this query of the Shōgunate distinctly
stated among other things the tendency of
the times which made it difficult to adhere
to the traditions of the land; and he also
proposed to rescind the law issued early in
the seventeenth century, prohibiting the
building of large vessels suitable for foreign
trade. He again advised the Shōgunate
to build navies for the protection of the
coasts. "Thus prepared," he writes, "the
country will be free from the menaces and
threatenings of foreign powers, and will be
able to uphold the national principle and
polity at any time." In preparing this
representation to the Yedo government,
the learned Nakagawa was his sole sup-

porter among the retainers of Hikoné. When Naosuké opened a conference with his followers before preparing his answer to the Shōgunate, it was found that all of them except Nakagawa were for exclusion. In opposition to the united opinion of his numerous followers, Naosuké saw truth in what Nakagawa said, and with his help he prepared the document to be sent to Yedo. This paper offers important proof of his advanced views even before he became Tairō.

Personally, Naosuké shared with men of his time the feeling of hatred toward foreigners. That which constitutes the main point of difference between him and his contemporaries lies in the fact that he kept his personal feelings entirely separate from the great problem of national interest.

It is not only the characteristic of the
politicians of Japan at that time, but of
those in all ages and countries also, that
they seldom draw a distinct line of separa-
tion between personal feelings and national
interest.   He who can do so, certainly
deserves the name of a great statesman.

The adoption of Nakagawa's view against
the so-called majority, goes to prove both
the strong will of Naosuké, and his clear
insight into the future of his country.   It
also proves his bravery and the profound
interest he felt for his country, for it is no
easy matter in any age to go against the
majority.   It is only clear foresight,
coupled with strong disinterested determina-
tion that enables one to act in defiance of
public opinion.   It is only in weaker and
more selfish hands that absolute power is

open to abuses.   Let it be bestowed upon
a man of Naosuké's type and character,
and it will not only be free from abuses,
but will help to open a new and decidedly
profitable career, otherwise closed.   However strongly one may denounce absolute
power, it has often proved to be a benefit
to a nation, as in the case of Ii Naosuké,
where great abilities and a disinterested
mind were united with clear insight into
the future of the whole nation.   Without
him the so-called majority might have
involved Japan in a policy not simply detrimental, but also dangerous to the interest and dignity of the whole empire.

CHAPTER III.

What has already been written will
clearly show to the reader that one of the
two great problems was that of opening the
country for foreign intercourse. The other
problem was the appointment of the Shōgun's Heir. The reigning Shōgun, Iyésada, had no male issue. It therefore
became necessary to appoint the Heir Apparent from one of the three Princely
families related to the Tokugawas, Mito,
Kii and Owari.

There were two candidates. One was
the Prince of Kii or Kishiu, and the other

was one of the sons of the Senior Prince of
Mito. The former was a mere boy, while
the latter was a young man already known
as a clever and able prince. He had been
adopted into the family of Hitotsubashi,*
and was then the Prince of that family.
When viewed from the side of blood
relationship to the Shōgun, he was more
distant than the young Prince of Kishiu,
but the party that would have him succeed
to the Shōgunate based their argument on
the necessity of the times. They said that
the crisis demanded a full grown able Shōgun, and that no better could be found
than the present Prince of Hitotsubashi.
Several of the powerful Barons favored

---

* Literally One Bridge. The name is perpetuated
in one of the great gates of the Castle or Shiro in
Tōkiō looking north upon the old grounds of the
Imperial University, G.

this view, while among the officers of the
Shōgunate, many were found who were of
this opinion. The other party dwelt on
the necessity of determining the Heirship
by nearness of blood relationship.

Iyésala, who was of a remarkably reserved nature, did not support the candidacy
of Prince Hitotsubashi. This Shōgun has
been taken for a weak-minded man. The
account given of him, however, by those
who were admitted into his confidence
fully contradict popular notions concerning
his intellectual capacities, and show clearly
that he was in full possession of at least
ordinary intelligence. He found himself
face to face with the double problem of
foreign intercourse and of appointing his
Heir. His Senators, the Rōju, with Baron
Abé at their head did not possess sufficient

strength to determine the question of opening the country to foreigners, and this lack of firmness finally resulted in the reference of the question to the Imperial Court and also to the Barons of the land. This was of course an entire departure from the usage of the Shōgunate, for in any political question, the decision of the Yedo government was at once final and absolute.

History clearly states that Prince Iyé-yasu, the founder of the line of the Toku-gawas, in the year 1613, entered into a commercial treaty with England, which, however, was given up on the part of the latter in 1625 because there was more loss* than profit in her trade with the Japan of

* £ 40.000

those days. This treaty was concluded
without any reference either to the Emperor or to the Barons.

Now, however, assailed by the question
of foreign intercourse, the Cabinet of the
Shōgunate under Iyésada, exposed its
weakness by refusing to make use of its
absolute power in political matters. A
forfeiture of absolute power is seldom
without a sudden outburst of conflicting
opinions, and this was exactly the case in
the time of agitated Japan.

By a strange coincidence, the Senior
Prince of Mito was at the head of the Exclusion Party as well as of the party supporting
the candidacy of his son, Prince Hitotsubashi. These two parties, though different
in name, were almost one and the same
under his leadership. Notwithstanding

his near relationship to the Shōgunate, as one of the Three Houses of the Tokugawa Family, Rekko proved to be a powerful political opponent of the Yedo administration. The very fact that the Shōgun's Senators or Cabinet advisers referred the question of commercial treaties to the Imperial Cabinet and to the Barons, proves that the former must have seen the impossibility of keeping Japan any longer in exclusion. If they saw that it was possible they would have taken the decided step of closing up the country, for they knew that they would be supported by the public opinion of the time. This departure from the clear precedents of the Shōgun's government was nothing short of an evasion of a responsibility in the face of a great problem.

Those who supported the candidacy of Prince Hitotsubashi were actuated by different motives. Some thought that his cleverness and ability being admitted on every side, he would be able to keep Japan insulated from foreign contact, and thus uphold the dignity and sacredness of the land.

Others wanted to strengthen the power of the Shōgunate by putting the man of universal popularity into the Shōgunal office. They hoped in this way to open the country to intercourse with foreign nations.

Others again knew the power and influence of the Senior Prince of Mito with the Imperial Cabinet and the Barons. They also knew that in Kiōto and among the Fudai Daimiō, the Shōgunate had

strong opponents. They reasoned therefore that by appointing Prince Hitotsubashi to the heirship, the two opposing
parties would be reconciled, since the can-
didate was a son of the powerful Prince of
Mito.

As already mentioned, the reigning Shōgun was not in favor of Prince Hitotsubashi, and yet he dared not openly express
his disapproval. His reserve was so great
as to make his officers believe that he had
formed no opinion in this matter. Further-
more, he did not like to offend the old
Prince of Mito, who naturally wished to
see his able son become virtual ruler of
the land.

The power of Mito party was growing
day by day, and some able men were sent
to Kiōto for the purpose of persuading the

Imperial Court to decide the question of heirship in behalf of Prince Hitotsubashi. The sole power of appointing the Heir, of course, rested with the reigning Shōgun, but before so strong an opposition, he dared not take a decided step.

One evening, Hiraoka, one of the confidential officers of the Shōgun, who is still living to bear witness of what is related here, found his master, Iyésada, unusually melancholy and morose. Hiraoka knew what was troubling him. He said that trustworthy help could be found in the person of Baron Ii Kamon-no-Kami Naosuké, and proposed to appoint him as the Tairō, which office the nature of the times so much required. Before this, the Shōgun must have heard of Naosuké's opinion through some of his Senators ; and he now made up his mind to vest the power of the government in the Baron of Hikoné whose family had always proved to be not only faithful but also possessed of ability ir itmes of need.

Baron Abé* who had long been the Senior of the Rōju or Senators, was at his own suggestion succeeded by Baron Hotta* whom he had nominated.

The warships of the United States that had come to Uraga in 1853, left Japan after a short stay, promising to come in the following year for a reply. Their re-appearance in 1854 was followed by the arrival of English ships, and also of Dutch and Russian vessels, with whom conventions for the relief of ships and sailors had

---

* Abé Isé no Kami, and Hotta Bitchiu no Kami are the full titles of these daimiō.

been concluded. But it was not until the arrival of the United States Consul-General, Mr. Townsend Harris, in 1856, that the question of foreign trade and residence began to assume a definite shape. After repeated interviews with local officers and agents sent from Yedo, and after many provoking delays of over fifteen months, the American Consul-General was admitted for the first time into the Castle of Yedo to present his credentials from the Government of Washington.*

Baron Hotta was now at the head of the Senators, and was the principal diplomatist of the country that had been closed up so long. The draft of a treaty was prepared

* See " Townsend Harris First American Minister to Japan," Atlantic Monthly, August 1892 ; also the " Townsend Harris" by Griffis.

with considerable modifications of that drafted the previous year.

The Japanese people of those days little knew the nature of that treaty. They had not the slightest idea of its commercial character. Consequently they mistook the American demand for the opening of Kanagawa, Yedo, Osaka, Hiogo, and Niigata for a scheme of territorial aggression. The result, as might be expected, was a still stronger opposition to the opening of the country to a foreign intercourse.

It was in the 12th month of the 4th year of Anséi era (1857) that after diplomatic interviews with the American representative, the Senators signed a representation to the Imperial Cabinet of Kiōto, stating the difficulty of exclusion, and a recommendation to conform to the necessity of

the times. The influence of the Exclusion
Party was such that no answer came even
in the first month of the following year.

Pressed on one side by Mr. Harris, the
American representative, and urged on the
other side by his anxiety for his country,
Baron Hotta now went in person to the
Imperial Capital. There he did his best in
explaining the impossibility of adhering to
the old tradition, but the influence of the
opposing party in Kiōto was too great.
The result was that he received instructions to consult further with the princes of
the Tokugawa Family and with the Barons
of the land, before again submitting the
question to the Imperial Cabinet.

This instruction from the Imperial
Court was next to a flat refusal of the
Shōgunate's proposal. On the 20th day of

the 4th month of the 5th year of Anséi era,
(June 2, 1858) Baron Hotta came back to
Yedo from his unsuccessful mission to the
Imperial City.

Thus the great question of making
treaties with foreign nations had reached
the climax of difficulty. None but a
master-mind could solve this problem ;
while the other, that of the appointment of
the Shōgun's heir, had also reached a
crisis which allowed of no delay.

The Shōgun now made up his mind.
On the 22nd day of the 4th month of the
same year, June 4, two days after the
return of Hotta from Kiōto, a private messenger was sent to the Yedo mansion of
Baron Ii. The Shōgun's wish was that
the lord of Hikoné should be Tairō.

On the following day the subject of this

biography was publicly installed into that high and responsible position, only next to that of the Shōgun himself. Ii was virtually master of the situation.

The tendency of the times daily increased the power and influence of Prince Rekko of Mito. The fact that he was an earnest advocate of the exclusion policy drew to him many adherents. His influence exerted on the question of the Shōgun's Heir proved to be a formidable offset to the other party led by the Baron of Hikoné.

CHAPTER IV.

THE TAIRŌ II SIGNS THE AMERICAN TREATY.

On the assumption of the great responsibility of Tairō Naosuké found himself face to face with the two great problems which had agitated the whole country during several years. The solution of both now centred in his own person.

As to the appointment of the Shōgun's Heir, Naosuké believed that the matter rested entirely with the Shōgun himself. He looked on the question as that with which the subjects had nothing to do. Iyésada had his own desire already formed, but as he was extremely reserved by nature, and since he knew that there were many powerful princes and barons in favor of Prince

Hitotsubashi, he dared not give any public expression to his feelings. In his new Tairō, however, he found a man who could carry out his wishes, and appoint as his heir the one on whom he had set his heart.

On the 1st day of the 6th month, 1858, (July 11) a little over a month after Nao-suké's installation into the office of Tairō preliminary notice of the appointment of the Prince of Kishiu as the Heir Apparent was given to Princes of the Tokugawa family* and to the Barons of the land.

---

* The Princes of Mito, Owari, and Kishiu were called Sanké or the Three Houses, while Princes Hitotsu-bashi, Tayasu, and Shimizu were denominated Sankiō, or the Three Princes. The first trio was created at the time when the Shōgunate was organized by Prince Iyéyasu. The other three were created afterward. They were branches of the Tokugawa family, and the former ranked higher than the latter. They might be called the Major and Minor Princes of Tokugawa blood.

The date of public or national announcement was fixed on the eighteenth day of
that month (July 29). The reason for
this procedure was that the matter had to
be presented for the Emperor's sanction,
which however was a mere formality.

In those days of imperfect means of
travelling, this period of eighteen days was
required for a messenger to go up to Kiōto
and bring back an answer. According to
calculation, the Imperial sanction would
reach Yedo on the 14th day of the same
month, if nothing occurred to prevent approval on the part of the Kiōto Cabinet.
In this case, however, the expected answer
did not come even on the 15th.

Here a word of explanation may be
necessary. The actual power of government was of course vested in the Shōgun,

but this did not nullify the sovereignty of
the Emperor who had his capital in the
city of Kiôto, where he had his own
Cabinet of Ministers and Counsellors.
There were several things which had to
receive the Imperial sanction, such as
appointment of the Shōgun's Heir, the
granting of official rank, etc. The rank
and title of the Shōgun himself had not
been self-assumed. Their only source was
in the Emperor himself and the Yedo
ruler was the Mikado's lieutenant. In the
course of two centuries and a half, the
lease of power by the Shōgunate had become so much like a permanent national
institution that in time Imperial requests
for sanction had settled into matters of
polite routine. Although the Emperor
had his own Cabinet, yet its Premier,

Ministers, Counsellors, etc. existed only in name. They had little or nothing to say against anything done by the Shōguns.

This style of government, called in history, Bunon Seiji, or government by the military class, originated with Yoritomo, about seven hundred years ago, and after meeting with several changes and vicissitudes, it had come down with constant increments of power to the days of the Tokugawas.*

Nevertheless, what had long been a shadow was now becoming a substance

---

* This duarchy was popularly spoken of as "The Throne and the Camp," the Mikado always having his court at Kiōto, the Shōgun holding the purse and sword in the east, first at Kamakura, (1192-1573) and then at Yedo (1603-1863). The families holding power in succession were the Minamoto (1192-1219), the Hōjō regents of the "puppet" Shōguns (1219-1333), the Ashikaga (1333-1574), and Tokugawas (1603-1868).

and the old body took on new life. Requests for imperial sanction ceased to be a
mere formality from the moment the question of foreign intercourse rose into view.
Henceforth the Kiōto Cabinet showed that
it would have a voice in the management
of state affairs. The Imperial Premier, or
Dai-Jō-Dai-Jin, Great Minister of the Great
Government was Prince Naotada.

The party of Prince Rekko, having
representatives in Kiōto, were busily engaged in influencing the Imperial Cabinet to
veto the policy pursued by the Yedo
government. The powerful princes and
barons who favored the views of Prince
Rekko, also made their influences felt on
the Kiōto Cabinet. The result of this
double pressure was that among the Kugé,
or Court nobles, several men of power and

influence sided with the opposition to the
Shōgunate.   The Imperial Premier, Prince
Naotada, however, was not influenced by
the opponents of the Yedo government,
and he was the only support among the
Imperial Cabinet on which Naosuké could
rely.

As to the question of making a treaty
with the American envoy, the party of exclusion which also supported the candidacy of Prince Hitotsubashi was busy in
making its influences felt on the Imperial
Cabinet.

Meanwhile the coming of the Mikado's
sanction was awaited with anxious suspense
at Yedo, but as it did not come, Naosuké
dispatched a special message to Kiōto.

Just at this unfortunate juncture, an
express message reached Yedo, that two

American men-of-war* had come to Shimoda, and that one of them proceeded up
the Bay of Yedo as far as Koshiba. This
was on the 13th day of the month. (July
24, 1858). On the 16th day, (July 27,)
another message came reporting an arrival
of Russian war-ships, and saying also that
they were soon to be followed by English
and French squadrons which had been
victorious in their war with China.

The Yedo government sent Governor
Inonyé and Overseer Iwasé to hold conference at Kanagawa with Mr. Harris, the
United States Consul-General at Shimoda.
In this conference Mr. Harris pointed out
the impossibility of exclusion, and the
danger attending adherence to the tradi-

---

* The U. S. S. S. Powhatan and Mississippi, Commodore Tatnall.

tional policy. The conference was closed by a request for speedy settlement of the treaty negotiations then under way. Assurances were given by the American representative of a friendly intervention in Japan's future intercourse with other powers of the West whereby she might obtain favorable terms with European nations.

The two commissioners returned to Yedo on the 19th day (July 30) to report the result of their interview with the representative of the United States. The Shōgunate now assembled its official advisers to discuss the great question which had been pending for several years. At this meeting they were all of opinion that the question had assumed such a form that only speedy settlement could save the nation from irreparable harm. Therefore, it would not only be better, but absolutely necessary, to act in the matter at once.

Here was the decisive moment not only in the history of the Tokugawa Shōgunate, but of Great Japan itself.

Shall Naosuké, by virtue of the power vested in him, decide the question before obtaining a formal sanction of the Imperial Cabinet ? The unsuccessful mission of Baron Hotta to the Imperial City was too recent an event to be forgotten by anybody. The renewed presentation of the same question would not only involve delays, but would surely meet with the same fate as on the former occasion. Naosuké believed that investment with the power of government carried with it the right to meet emergencies according to the judgment of

the person so invested. He also knew
that the national safety and dignity were
involved in this question. He therefore
decided to assume the entire responsibility.

No sooner was the decision made than
he immediately dispatched Inouyé and
Iwasé to Kanagawa, authorizing them to
sign the provisional treaty which has since
been called the Temporary Kanagawa
Treaty, which was to be subject to revision
after a specified term of years, but which
has never been changed in spite of the tens
of years that have since elapsed, even after
the point of time designated.*

On the 21st day of the same month,
(August 1st) Prince Rekkō wrote a letter to
the Tairō Naosuké, stating his anxiety as

---

* The ratification of the revised Treaty with the
United States took effect as late as this year (1895).

to the conduct of the Shōgunate in the
question of foreign intercourse. He also
clearly stated the inadvisability of taking
the decisive step of signing the treaty before
the Imperial sanction was received. He
advised that the acts of the Shōgunate be
limited to what was unavoidable and then
to dispatch either the Tairō or some of the
Senators as a messenger to Kiōto to lay
the matter before the Throne. Among
other things he again clearly expressed his
disapproval of permitting residence on the
soil to the ministers of foreign nations or
of allowing their nationals to trade.

According to the tenor of his letter, the
Prince himself must have been aware of
the impossibility of utter exclusion, for he
advises the Yedo Cabinet to limit its conduct
to " such parts as are entirely unavoidable."

Hence the difference between him and the Tairō may be considered as resting on the one point of "before" or "after" the coming of the Imperial sanction. Even in the time of Baron Hotta it had been impossible to obtain this, and now that the influence of Prince Rekko and the Exclusion Party had so increased, little success could be expected when the question should be brought before the Imperial Cabinet. Meanwhile procrastination at Kiōto might have involved the whole country in serious consequences and irremediable calamities. Naosuké knew too well the kind of difficulty into which China had involved herself. He was prepared to risk his life rather than to see his country plunged in similar miseries which moreover might be attended with national shame.

On the 22nd day, (August 2) the Tairō dispatched a message to Kiōto stating the impossibility of closing up the country to foreign intercourse, as well as the trouble and danger attending the exclusion. At the same time he gave assurances that the Shōgunate would do its utmost to protect the coasts and insure safety for the whole land.

On the same day, the Princes and Barons were summoned to the Castle of Yedo, where the conduct of the Shōgunate in reference to the treaty with the United States was publicly notified. The tenor of the notification was similar to that of the report sent to Kiōto except the one clause which required them to state their views to the government in reference thereto. On the 23rd day, Naosuké himself wrote an answer to Prince Rekko, thanking him for his kind advice, but regretting his inability to follow his counsel owing to the unavoidable nature of the case in hand. He also fully stated the circumstances, asking the Prince's sympathy with him in the serious and difficult position in which he was now placed. He also humbly expressed his lack of ability for so important a post at such a crisis, and requested the Prince of Mito to oblige him with further counsels for the sake of the nation at large.

On this very same day, (23rd) the Imperial sanction for appointing the Prince of Kishiu to the Heir Apparent of the Shōgun was received from Kiōto. It was dated the 8th day, (July 19) and all other correspondences from Kiōto under the same date reached Yedo on the 14th day (July 25).

Why was this one document containing the Imperial sanction delayed so long? In all probability it must have been purposely kept back by some of the opposition party with a view to effect their own end, yet, as it proved, without success.

A few days after this, the Chief of the Privy Recorder, Shiga, through whose hand the paper reached the Tairō, committed suicide. Nobody could explain his death at that time, but it was said to be in order to escape the punishment attending the withholding of the Imperial sanction.

The 25th day (August 6) had been fixed for the public announcement of the appointment of the Heir Apparent. But the Princes of Mito and Owari, and Baron

Matsudaira of Echizen * as well as those
of the same opinion with them still tried
hard to have Prince Hitotsubashi appointed
as the Heir.

On this day, changes took place in the
Yedo Cabinet. The two Senators, Baron
Hotta and Baron Matsudaira, were succeeded in their office by Barons Ota, Matsudaira of Nishiwo, and Manabé. The
reason of the change was because Baron
Hotta had lost the Shōgun's confidence on
account of his unsuccessful mission to
Kiōto, while Baron Matsudaira favored the
candidacy of Prince Hitotsubashi.

The moment the conclution of the Temporary Treaty was made public, the exclu-

---

* For a portrait of this enlightened daimiō and
notice of his life, see The Mikado's Empire,
pp. 308,6)9.

sion party began to show an increased
vehemence in their opposition. Baron
Matsudaira of Echizen called on the Tairō
Naosuké in his mansion and a long discussion took place, but before coming to any
conclusion, the latter had to excuse himself,
much to the former's dissatisfaction, for the
hour came for him to go to the Court.

This was on the 24th day (August 4).
On the same day, the Senior and Junior
Princes of Mito, together with the Prince
of Owari, suddenly presented themselves
to the Castle or the Shōgun's Court. Baron
Matsudaira of Echizen, hearing of this
sudden visit of the three Princes also followed them to the Castle. In this era,
there were certain days fixed for the appearance of respective Princes and Barons
at the Shōgun's Castle, or they were

required to give due notice of so doing.
This sudden visit of the three Princes was
wholly contrary to the rule and usage of
the times. The officers of the Court were
naturally taken by surprise and when the
matter was brought before the Cabinet.
the Senator Baron Manabé said to the
Tairō that the meaning of the sudden
appearance of the three Princes was more
than clear. The person whom they looked
upon as the principal opponent being the
Tairō, it would be better for the Senators
to see the visitors without Naosuké, lest his
presence should involve the matter in a
serious complication.

Naosuké replied that his failure to see
them, the Princes of Mito, and Owari.
would be taken for timidity. and that the

The meeting of the leaders of two oppo

(2)   The Tairō Ii Naosuké.

: parties in the Great Parlor of Yedo Castle.
　　(1)　Prince Rekkō of Mito.

official dignity of the Tairō required him not to avoid this meeting.

The three Princes, two of Mito, and one of Owari, were admitted to the Hall of Audience where high dignitaries alone are permitted to come. The Lord of Echizen remained in an ante-room near by. Now took place one of the great events in the history of Anséi era (1854-1859). A rumor flew fast and wide that the Princes of Mito and Owari had suddenly appeared at the Castle to convince Naosuké of his great mistake and to require him to commit *seppuku* * for his conduct.

The leaders of the two rival parties having now met face to face, nothing short of a hot discussion could be expected.

---

* The more elegant Chinese Term for " belly-cutting " or hara-kiri.

The debate was opened with the question of foreign intercourse. Prince Rekkō blamed Naosuké for concluding the American treaty before the Imperial sanction had been received. But when the Tairō explained the irrepressible tendencies of the times and professed his confidence of meeting with Imperial approval under the circumstances, this subject could not be pressed any further.

The three Princes then began to show the need of the times for a full-grown able prince for the Shōgun's heir. They said that none would be better qualified than Prince Hitotsubashi. To this, Naosuké simply replied that the right of appointing the Heir Apparent rested solely with the Shōgun, and this rule left no room for any of his relations or of subjects to say aught against what he had appointed. He also stated that the matter of heirship having been already settled, and being ready for formal announcement on the following day (25th), it would be improper now to further discuss that affair.

Prince Rekkō thereupon advised the Tairō to withhold the announcement of heirship for a time and thus manifest a proper sense of respect and deference toward the Imperial Cabinet, especially after the conduct of the Shōgunate in concluding the American treaty before obtaining the Emperor's order.

Naosuké's reply was that he had perfect confidence that the matter would meet with the Emperor's approval, and that the long vacancy of the Shōgun's heirship being against the Imperial will, he could not follow the advice of the Prince.

" Why does not Your Excellency dispatch a messenger to Kiōto to explain the circumstances attending the conclusion of the treaty ?" was the next question of Prince Rekkō.

Naosuké answered that it had already been decided to send Senator Baron Manabé to Kiōto, and that his official instructions would be given him on the following day.

The last subject which Prince Rekkō brought up was his advice to appoint the Baron of Echizen to the office of the Tairō, * to which Naosuké replied that in this question he was entirely powerless.

At this point the timely wit of Baron

---

* Matsudaira, Lord of Echizen was appointed Tairō in 1862.

Manabé caused both parties, bitter rivals though they were, to close their interview amid unexpected laughter on both sides. Manabé's joke was this : " The number of the Honorable Houses of Tokugawa, besides the Shōgun, is limited to three, how can anybody make the number four. There is only one office of Tairō, and I cannot see how it can be made into two." When written down or translated, the reason of the fun is not evident, yet the effect was powerful. Evidently the witticism must have been uttered in a way only known to the practiced joker.

During this interview Prince Rekkō called aloud for Baron Matsudaira of Echizen, but Naosuké objected on the ground that his official standing did not entitle him to a place in the Hall of

Audience.   He also objected to the request
of the Prince of Owari to have an interview
with the Shōgun, on the ground that the
latter was too ill to see anybody.

Whatever enmity might have lurked in
the breast of those men present at this
interview, the gathering was brought to a
peaceful close.   Matsudaira of Echizen who
was not admitted to the presence of the
Tairō held a conference with Senator
Baron Manabe, and after expressing the
same views as those of Prince Rekkō, also
retired from the Court.

CHAPTER V.

THE CONSEQUENCES.

The double problem which had so long
agitated the whole country found complete
solution at the hand of the Tairō Naosuké, but the feelings of enmity and opposition created by his acts suffered no abate-
ment.

The question of heirship not being so
open to discussion as the other, the force of
the Opposition Party was now concentrated
on the question of the treatment of foreigners. The Opposition attacked Naosuké's policy of concluding the treaty before
obtaining the Emperor's formal sanction.
They condemned him for an act which,
according to their views, was disobedience
to the Imperial will.

Now the whole question turns on this point : was the conclusion of the treaty disobedience to the Emperor, or was there sufficient reason authorizing Naosuké to reverse the order of routine and formality in this affair ?

Those who condemn Naosuké's policy build their argument on the fact that he went *against* the Imperial will by signing the American treaty before obtaining sanction from Kiōto. But whatever may be said, there is nothing to show that Naosuké disobeyed the Imperial order, for the Cabinet of Kiōto never expressly gave orders that the country should be closed to oreign nations. All the instruction given, went no farther than to require further conference among the Princes, Officers, and Barons of the land. To any impartial

judge, this fact will clearly exonerate
Naosuké from the serious charge of disobedience to the Imperial instruction.
Further, when the tendencies of the times
are fully considered, it will also establish
his disinterested love for his country.
Failure to carry out an instruction and
wilful disobedience are two things that
must never be confounded.

Shōgunate did not open a conference
with the Princes and Barons as required
by the Imperial instruction that Baron
Hotta had received at Kiōto. Under the
circumstances already narrated, the Tairō
did not call a council of the Daimiō.
Since the Tairō had substantial reasons
for changing the traditional and formal
order of procedure, he is not only ex-
onerated from the charge of disobedience,

but it is seen that the nature of power
vested in him authorized him to abide by
his own judgment, especially when he saw
clearly that it was in the national interests
so to act.

Indeed it is not too much to say that
without Naosuké's bravery and clear foresight, Japan, now in the full enjoyment of
the enlightened Méiji era, would not have
realized a career of progress so smooth,
peaceful, and rapid, nor have taken so great
strides in politics, science, and social im-
provements such as those we witness to-
day.

Another party threw blames not only on
Naosuké, but also on the United States
representative, Mr. Townsend Harris.
They asserted that the latter used threats
in forcing Japan to enter into a treaty with

the United States, and that Naosuké was
compelled to do as he was dictated to by
the American representative.

The merit of this view will become apparent when one examines the nature of the
so-called threats. " Were they founded on
truth, or were they mere words of menace
which had no foundation in truth? " History proves that China fought against the
allied forces of France and England, and
that her bigotted adherence to the policy of
exclusion resulted not only in her defeat,
but also in giving a part of her dominion
to the conqueror. A diplomat who should
carry out the instructions of his government could not be blamed for availing himself of any occurrence that might help him
to forward the cause of his mission. When,
moreover, it is clear that whatsoever the

United States representative said was based on a friendly feeling, there is little room for criticism of Mr. Harris's attitude toward the then government of Dai Nippon.

On the 25th day (6th month) the appointment of the Prince of Kishiu, aged thirteen years, to be Heir Apparent to the Shōgun was publicly announced.

On the 2nd day of the 7th month, (August 11), the formal congratulations of the Barons were presented in person, and were received at the Castle in Yedo by the Shōgun, and his Heir, whose name was Iyémochi. On the night of this auspicious day, the Shōgun was suddenly taken ill, and on the following day, his illness became serious.

On the 4th day, he felt a little better

and calling the Tairō and Senators to his room, the mighty problem of how to deal with the Princes of Mito and Owari, and also of the Baron Matsudaira of Echizen, was decided, the result of which was made known on the following day. The Senior Prince of Mito was ordered to confinement in a separate mansion, the Prince of Owari and the Baron of Echizen were ordered to retire from active duty and transfer the government of their territories to their respective heirs. The Prince of Mito and Prince Hitotsubashi were suspended from the privilege of presenting themselves at the Shōgun's Court or Castle.

On the 6th day, (August 15), an order was received from Kiōto, requiring either the Tairō or one of the Princes of the

Three Houses of Tokugawa to appear at the Imperial Court in reference to the question of foreign intercourse.

On the night of the same day the Shōgun breathed his last.

Two days before this, (on 4th), three English ships arrived at Shinagawa, a suburb of Yedo, while the Russians came into the city itself and took up their temporary abode in one of the Buddhist temples.

So many things of serious importance came up in so short a time, that all was confusion in the offices of the Shōgunate. Each officer had more business than he could transact. The state of affairs was so complicated that it was enough to bewilder minds of ordinary capacity.

Placed in the midst of these complica-

tions, Naosuké dispatched Senator Baron
Ota to hold a conference with the British
representative,* with whom the business
was facilitated by the previous treaty with
the United States. A messenger was sent
to Kiōto at the same time, stating the circumstances which made it impossible to
comply with the Imperial order. A still
more important line of business lay in preparing against emergencies that might
follow the sentences of condemnation pro-
nounced on the Great Princes and the
Baron of Echizen.

It has been stated that the Shōgunate
intended to dispatch Senator Baron
Manabé to Kiōto to explain its conduct
toward the United States. A paper had

---

* See Chapter V. Vol. Ii of Laurence Oliphant's
Lord Elgin's Mission to China and Japan.

been prepared for that purpose but owing
to the death of the Shōgun, the appointed
messenger was prevented from going up,
and the paper alone was sent to the Premier
Naotada for his perusal. The substance of
the document was as follows :

" The question of foreign intercourse is
pregnant with serious consequences. The
reason why the treaty was concluded with
the United States was because of the case
requiring an immediate answer. The
English and French squadrons after their
victory over China were very soon expected
to our coasts, and the necessity of holding
conferences with different nations at the
same time might cause confusion from
which little else than war could be expected. These foreigners are no longer to
be despised. The art of navigation, their

steam-vessels, and their military and naval preparations have found full development in their hands. A war with them might result in temporary victories on our part, but when our country should come to be surrounded by their combined navies, the whole land would be involved in consequences which are clearly visible in China's experience. This question of foreign intercourse had been referred to the Barons, and most of them knew the disadvantage of war with foreigners. Under these circumstances no other recourse was found than to conclude a treaty and open some of the ports to them for trade. Trying this policy for ten or twelve years, and making full preparation for protection of the country during that period, we can then determine whether to close up

or open the country to foreign trade and
residence. To commit the nation to the
policy of exclusion before any experiment,
appears to be highly inadvisable. If it
were only one nation with which we had
to deal, it would be much easier, but
several nations, coming at the same time
with their advanced arts, it is entirely impossible to refuse their requests to open
intercourse with our country. The tendency of the times makes exclusion an
entire impossibility. Compliance with
their requests will tend to bring safety to
the whole land, and thus we shall be able
to keep His Majesty free from cares and
anxieties for his subjects."

The paper also stated the advisability of
opening Hiōgo, to which there had been an

objection because of its nearness to the
Imperial Capital.

A careful examination of the original
document shows that special attention was
given to the use of words, in order not to
enter into collision with anti-foreign prejudices. To state the power and strength
of Western nations without reserve, would
certainly wound the pride of the politicians
and yet the thing could not be kept entirely
covered up. The only way was to clothe the
circumstances with the words " unavoidable," and " tendency of the times." The
unsuccessful mission of Baron Hotta before
the Kiōto Cabinet was said to have been
mainly due to his unreserved description
of the power of the Western nations. Instead of convincing the party of opposition
the unavoidable nature of the case, Baron

Hotta's representation had only served to kindle their blind prejudices, and thus make his mission entirely fruitless.

Such was the feeling of those days. Even those who knew the strength of foreign nations, would not dare to fully express their knowledge, lest they should be misunderstood. The paper also distinctly shows an unfriendly feeling toward foreigners, and this was again a marked feature of those days. An expression of friendliness to a foreign nation would only have stirred up prejudices, and made intercourse with Western nations more and more difficult.

The death of the Shōgun Iyésada was publicly announced on the 8th day of 8th month (September 15), and Prince Tayasu was appointed to the regency of the young heir Iyémochi.

By this time, the alienation between the Shōgunate and the Prince of Mito became more and more serious. The former kept a strict watch over the actions of the latter, and the residence of Prince Rekkō was guarded by the officers of the Shōgunate. In Kiōto also, the friction between the two parties grew day by day. The Yedo party was led by the Premier Prince Naotada, while the anti-foreign party had a leader in Prince Takatsukasa who was one of the Imperial Councillors, and possessed several influential adherents both in and out of the Imperial Cabinet.

The victory or defeat of either of the two parties seemed to rest in the instructions from His Majesty, the Emperor, but

so long as Naotada held the Chancellorship
and Naosuké the office of Tairō, their joint
power was well established, for any instructions from the Emperor must necessarily
pass through the hand of the Premier.

Once it appeared that the Premier was
going to lose his power, for his opponent
Prince Takatsukasa almost prevailed on
him to resign, but the tidings of the public
announcement of the Shōgun's death, and
the installation of the young heir under the
regency of Prince Tayasu, encouraged him
to continue in the office, for he saw thereby
that Naosuké was resolute and unflinching
in his policy, in spite of strong opposition.

Among the Imperial Councillors and
gentry of Kiōto, however, the influence of
Prince Rekkō was as strong as ever.   The
loss of his power in Yedo being nothing

short of the decadence of the influence of
his party in Kiōto, the Imperial instruction
requiring the presence of either the Tairō
or one of the Princes of the Three Houses
of Tokugawa, was issued, in order to
strengthen the power of the Exclusion
Party. The Premier tried to stop the
issue of this order, but in vain.

Naosuké knew, however, that should he
go up to Kiōto to discuss the question, he
would place himself at the mercy of his
opponents, and that the final result would
be the reversal of the policy already taken
by the Shōgunate. An extraordinary pressure of business at this time, supplied him
with a laudable excuse for his non-appear-
ance, while the confinement of the Princes
of Mito and Owari, and the youth of the
Prince of Kishiu prevented any of the full-

grown Princes from going up to the Imperial City.

Failing in their attempt to call Naosuké to Kiōto, and learning that Senator Baron Manabé was coming in his place, the bitter feeling of the Exclusion Party against the Tairō increased all the more, nor were they idle in the meantime.   They took advantage of the Premier's absence on account of illness, and managed to draw up two Imperial instructions, one to the Shōgunate and the other to the Prince of Mito.   The tenor of the instruction to the former was disapproval of opening the country to foreign intercourse, and it also required an explanation of the failure of any of the Tokugawa Princes, or the Tairō, to come to Kiōto as commanded in the previous instruction.

This Imperial paper was received on the 18th day of the 8th month (September 25), and on the same day a notice was received from the Prince of Mito that he had been honored with direct instructions from His Majesty. Strangely enough, this document for Prince Mito reached him one day earlier than the one furnished to the Shōgunate. In Kiōto the paper was delivered through one of the Court Councillors to Ukai, the representative of Prince Mito, whose men immediately left Kiōto, and travelling privately reached the Yedo mansion of Prince Mito before the regular bearer of the Imperial paper to the Shōgunate arrived in the same city.

The Prince of Mito being yet in his confinement, was not allowed to come to the Court, and the two Senators, Barons

Ōta and Manabé, were dispatched to the Prince's mansion to see the Imperial document.   It was found to be almost the same with the one received by the Shō-gunate.

This direct granting of an Imperial communication to any other than the Shōgunate was a serious departure from long established usage.   The Senior Prince of Mito of course knew how it came, but the Junior Prince did not know the secret of its origin.   Afterward learning that only the instruction to the Shōgunate had been accompanied by a document from the Court Officials, assuring that no contention existed between the Imperial Cabinet and the Shōgunate, he asked the two Senators as to what he should do.   The moment he had received the communication from

Kiōto he felt uneasy as to the course he should pursue, for should he keep the matter secret from the Shōgunate, it would be a disregard of the Imperial order. On the other hand, should he make these facts known to the Shōgunate, he would expose himself to the suspicion of secret treachery toward the Yedo government. Hence his asking the judgment of the two Senators as to the proper course he should take. Their answer was that they should consult with the Tairō about his question.

On the 22nd day (September 29), a letter was received from one of Naosuké's confidential men, saying that the Premier's absence had been taken advantage of by his enemies, and that the Premier found it too late to stop the Imperial instruction already drawn up. The letter also stated

that the Premier was awaiting the arrival
of Baron Manabé in order to initiate proper
measures to counteract the artifices of the
other party.   This piece of news hurried
the departure of the Baron, and on the
2.)th day, (October 6) Naosuké held conference with the Senators as to the tenor
of the message to be forwarded to Kiōto.
He drew up a lengthy paper stating the
circumstances of the situation in detail.
Baron Manabé, however, was inclined to
leave the greater part of the case to a
verbal explanation, and as he was the person to represent the Shōgunate, his suggestion was adopted.   He left Yedo on his
important mission on the 3rd day of the 9th
month (October 10).

The relation between the Shōgunate
and the Party of Exclusion may well be

likened unto that of fire and water. The
antagonistic feeling had almost reached its
acme. It was ready to burst out on the
slightest occasion. A secret message of
the Exclusion Party to one of the Karō
or Elders of the Mito Clan, dated 15th of
9th month (October 22), was intercepted
by one of Naosuké's detectives. The letter
strongly advised personal violence against
Baron Ii Naosuké. In this way it was
hoped that his power would be crippled
and Prince Rekkō be released from confinement.

A comet appeared at the time and out of
superstition grew many stories, which were
more or less indicative of the spirit of the
times.

In the view most prevalent, a serious
rebellion was anticipated. Hitherto hos-

tilities between the two parties had proceeded no farther than obstruction. Now,
however, the power of the Exclusion Party
had assumed a threatening aspect. Their
audacity went so far as to persuade the
Premier Prince Naotada to resign his
office. They saw that the arrival of Baron
Manabe in Kiōto marked the critical
moment in the history of both parties and
they tried to undermine the power of the
Shōgunate by pulling down the only support it had in the Imperial Cabinet. The
Premier had to yeild to their persuasion,
and notified of his intention to resign.

This serious news reached Yedo after
Baron Manabé had left the city for Kiōto,
and the Tairō was utterly ignorant of what
had occurred. Nothing surprised Naosuké more than this report. He im-

mediately dispatched a message to over-
take Baron Manabé, in which he instructed
him to take advantage of the absence of
Imperial permission to the Premier's proposed resignation. A mere application to
resign did not release any one from his
official duties. He also gave instructions
that business should be transacted only
through the Premier.

The increasing influence of the other
party, and the threatening attitude they
began to assume, prompted Naosuké to
take decisive measures againt those in
Kiōto who were active against the policy
of the Shōgunate. He ordered the arrest
of Uméda, Ukai, and his son, who had
done their utmost to subvert the political
measure of the Yedo government. Many
others were also arrested and thus their

strength in the Imperial City was con-
siderably reduced.   •

This act of Naosuké forms the part of
his political career most vulnerable to criticism. While the nature of the power
invested in him, and the need of the times
authorized him to resort to these severe
measures, it cannot be denied that this act
of his resulted in a loss of many of the able
and brave men of the country. This is an
indispensable side of any political change,
yet when one considers the greatness of
the revolution, which Japan was beginning
to undergo, her loss of able men seems
comparatively small.

It was on the 10th day of the 9th month
(October 17). that Baron Manabé arrived
in Kiōto. His time was at first spent in
suppression of the power of his political

opponents.   His energetic movements pro-
duced so remarkable a change in the state
of things in the Imperial City, that Prince
Nijō who was one of those who had per-
suaded Naotada the Premier to resign,
now entirely changed his attitude.   He
met the Premier on the 8th day of the
10th month and advised him to withdraw
his application for resignation which had
been kept in abeyance since the 9th month.
On the 15th day, Naotada was honored
with a letter from His Majesty, the Emperor Kōmei, encouraging him to continue
in his office as Premier.

Naotada could desire nothing more and
he began to attend the Cabinet meetings
from the 19th day, the political situation in
Kiōto undergoing a still greater change in
favor of the Shōgunate.

The Exclusion Party had built the citadel of their resistance in oppsition to the opening of Hiōgo as a treaty port, and so made it difficult to carry out the purpose of the Shōgunate in this matter. The re-instatement of Prince Naotada however opened a way to explain the conduct of the Shōgunate in reference to foreign affairs. Baron Manabé presented himself at the Imperial Court on the 24th day of the 10th month, (November 30) to offer explanations, his success being at once apparent.

On the following day the formal in-auguration of Iyémochi to the office of Shōgun was issued by the Emperor, and Prince Nijō was appointed as the bearer of this Imperial message to the Castle of Yedo.*

On the 1st day of the 12th month (January 4, 1859), Iyéshigé formally received this Imperial investiture through the hand of Prince Nijō.

On the last day of the same month, (February 3, 1859) an Imperial answer in reference to foreign affairs was received by Baron Manabé in which it was stated that the said question had been a constant source of anxiety to His Majesty, in as much as it concerned a departure from a long tradition, and also the dignity of the Empire, but the unavoidable circumstance

* The right of inaugurating any person to the office of Shōgun was reserved in the Emperor, and every new Shōgun had to receive a formal appointment from the Emperor to that office, through a special messenger sent down from Kiōto.

of the times having been fully recognized
by His Majesty, and the intention of the
Shōgunate to resume the policy of exclusion having been assured, time is granted
for that purpose, and the Shōgun is
authorized to take temporary measures to
suit the requirements of the present time.

The granting of this instruction had
come after one hundred and three days
from the arrival of Baron Manabe in Kiōto,
during which time highest order of eloquence and wisdom had been engaged to
secure this deliverance from the Throne.

Those leaders of the Opposition who had
been arrested were sent down to Yedo for
examination. They reached the eastern
city on the 29th day of the 12th month
(February 3, 1859). A Special Court was
opened for their trial, and they were dealt

with in accordance with the laws of those
days. The ringleaders were sentenced to
capital punishment, while minor offenders
were banished to respective islands.

This action of the Tairō called down on
him the vilest names and malicious epithets
that could be invented. They naturally
came from the sympathizers of those politicians who were very numerous in those
days. What they wrote forms a large part
of the Anséi literature. The name of Naosuké came to be identified by many with
that of a proud and selfish autocrat of the
worst type.

Yet when we judge him by the standard
of his age, when political liberty was next
to unknown, it would be clear to any
impartial judge that this action of Naosuké
was based, not on his personal enmity, but

on sincere love for his country and on his firm confidence in the advantage of the policy to be followed. It is often by a painful surgical operation that a serious injury and danger to life is avoided. Naosuké's purpose in punishing some of the notorious ringleaders of the Exclusion Party was in order to save the whole land from a dangerous agitation, which might result in an irremediable mistake.

The granting of this latest order from the Emperor was a signal victory of Naosuké's party, and Baron Manabé came back to Yedo on the 15th day of the 3rd month, (April 18, 1859). Now that the ringleaders of the Opposition had been dealt with, the question was what to do with the Imperial instruction sent to the Prince of Mito. Another question was whether to publicly

announce the last order from Kiōto, or to
keep it officially secret. How to deal with
the Imperial Ministers and Councillors in
the Exclusion Party was also a question of
the times, but before any decided measure
was taken by the Shōgunate, Prince Takatsukasa and his son, and Princes Konoyé
and Sanjō resigned.

The Imperial instructions, however,
allowed merely a temporary opening of
the country. Naosuké being fully con-
vinced of the impossibility of entire
exclusion, now endeavored to obtain
unqualified sanction of the Emperor to foreign intercourse. In order to accomplish
this end, he tried by every means to cement
the relation between the Imperial Court
and the Shōgunate. Not for his personal
aggrandizement but for the good of the

Empire, he purposed to prevent the extension of any counteracting influence on the Kiōto Cabinet. Hence he proposed the granting of Her Imperial Highness, Princess Kazu, in marriage to the young Shōgun. This was a political marriage which Naosuké effected in order to guard against future differences between the two courts, of Kiōto and Yedo. Although this marriage took place after the death of the Tairō,* yet it was the fruit of his labors in increasing and cementing the amicable relation between the Mikado and his lieutenant. Thus strengthening the basis of the whole duarchy, Naosuké tried gradually

---

* The Princess Kazu, aunt of the present Emperor, received the title of Kazu Miya and Princess of the Blood July 5, 1861. She arrived in Yedo and was married in December to the young Shōgun.

to effect the political purposes he had in view.

As to the public announcement of the last orders from Kiōto, there was a difference of opinion between the Tairō and Baron Manabé, who said that it would be necessary to obtain permission from the Premier before the instruction could be published. The matter was kept in abeyance, but this difference together with some other causes, finally resulted in the latter's resignation in the 12th month of that year, 1859.

Now the question demanding immediate attention related to the Imperial instruction sent to the Prince of Mito. The whole power of government had been conferred on the Shōgunate since the time of its organization in 1603, and an Imperial instruction on political matters sent to a person other than the Shōgun, was detrimental to the sole right of government vested in him.

A conference with the Imperial Cabinet resulted in a new order to the Prince of Mito, requiring him to return the instruction. The opinions of the Clansmen of Mito, however, were strongly divided on this point. One party said that the Imperial instruction should not be given up, and that the new order sent to the Clan must be a cunning artifice of the Shōgunate which could not have its origin in the Emperor himself, while the other party approved of quietly returning the paper in compliance with the new order.

The differences of the two factions went so far as an appeal to the sword. The

former party actually armed themselves
and camped out in order to stop the messenger that might be sent to receive the
paper. The whole territory of the Prince
of Mito was in a state of great agitation.
Some of their eminent men who advocated
the returning of the paper were assassinated on the street, and on one occasion the
party of those who would not give up the
paper, assembled in a body and fought
against a band of soldiers sent down to dis-
perse them. It was after some loss of
lives on both sides that they were finally
driven away.

This state of affairs must have been
occasioned by the strong feeling of enmity
entertained by many of the clansmen
against Naosuké who held the whole power
of the Shōgunate, and opposed the policy of

Prince Rekkō. It was on the 17th day of the 12th month (1859), that the Shōgunate officially informed the Prince of Mito of the order from Kiōto requiring him to return the Imperial instruction given him. Baron Andō was the bearer of this message.

On the 16th day of the 1st month (February 8, 1859), the Prince sent one of his Elders with an escort to the city of Mito, about twenty-five leagues north-west of Yedo. These were instructed to bring back the Imperial paper, but when they arrived at a place about four miles from the Castle of Mito, they found their way blocked by an armed band of the other party. They could not make them open a way for them, so they had to come back to Yedo without fulfilling their mission.

The party opposed to the return of the

Imperial order, fearing that the paper might be secretly stolen away, concealed it in the sacred building in the cemetery of Mito Princes.

All that could now be done under the circumstances by the Prince of Mito was to ask the Shōgunate for an extension of time. Matters continued in this state for some months, during which time some drew up a memorial stating the absence of reason for returning the paper with which the clan had once been honored, while others resorted to force to keep the paper in their clan.

Time went on in this state, and in the 3rd month (March, 1860) the paper could not be received back, for on the 3rd day of that month, the Tairō Naosuké on his way to the Shōgur's Court, was suddenly attacked by a band of assassins and met a cruel death at their hands.

Thus ended the short but brilliant career of one of the greatest statesmen of the East. At the risk of his personal safety he had broken the thick ice of exclusion and opened this country to the civilization of the 19th century. The hard ice once broken, Japan has made giant strides in her advancement within only thirty years. She now enjoys a perfect peace and unrestrained progress under a sound constitutional government, presided over by the Emperor of an unbroken lineage of nearly three thousand years.*

Naosuké was forty-six years old when this sad event cut him off, but according to

---

* Traditionally from 660 B. C., historically from the fifth century. G.

the orders of the Shōgunate, his death was
not announced until the last day of the
following month. It was given out that
he was wounded. To keep up appearances,
formal messengers from the Shōgun's Castle
were frequently sent to the mansion, no-
minally to inquire after his health.

This year, 1861, was a leap-year and had
an intercalary period, making two months
of the same name, that is the third. The
Tairō's death, when publicly announced was
officially dated on the last day of the second
3rd month (May 21, 1860). In those days,
and until 1872, the Lunar calendar was
used. Every leap-year used to have thirteen months, the duplication of the month
differing in each year according to the
calculation of the Yedo astronomers. The
dead Tairō was buried (May 30th) in

the ground of the Temple Gotokuji in
Sédagaya village near Yedo, beside the
tombs of his predecessors. Eight sons
and eight daughters survived him. The
eldest son having died young, the second
son, Naonori, succeeded, who was made
a Count by the present Emp ror, when he
established the five orders of peerage
The present master of this historical family
is Count Ii Naonori,* the second son of
the martyr of a policy which gave a new
life to an old country isolated for hundreds
of years.

---

* Educated in Brooklyn N.Y.

Baron Matsudaira pursuadin[

he Tairō to resign his office.

CHAPTER VI.

THE ASSASSINATION.

The 3rd day of the 3rd month (March 25) was one of the five annual festivals, when the Princes and Barons of the land had to present themselves at the Shōgun's Castle to offer congratulations of the occasion. Being the last month of Spring, it is usually not cold, but on this special day nature seemed to portend by an unusual phenomenon the dark event which was to make it a black day in the annals of Japan. She seemed to show her sympathy for the heavy loss about to fall upon the whole empire; for instead of a bright clear day, the sky was overcast with gloomy clouds, the temperature was exceptionally low, and

snow began to fall thick and heavy. The
smiles of nature on mountains and plains
were completely veiled from view by this
untimely visitor from midwinter. The
snow-flakes fell so thickly that objects but
a few yards off could not be distinctly seen.

It was the custom whenever a Prince or
Baron went out in public to be accompanied
by an extended following. On festival
occasions the procession was especially
large. The brilliant body-guards were
dressed in a light jaunty style, and were
armed with two bright swords in handsomely lacquered scabbards, which combined artistic taste with practical use. The most
prominent feature of the procession was
the *Kago*, or palanquin, carried on men's
shoulders within which the Daimiō was
seated. The insignia and blazonry of the

various feudal families made a brave display.
These consisted of crests, spears, horse-
decorations, and various emblems peculiar
to Japanese heraldry. These always
preceded the cortege proper.

Immediately following came the second
division. The *Kago* was borne in the
middle with personal guards attendant on
each side. The rear was brought up by
other retainers and guards. At the Castle
men expert in recognizing the heraldic
insignia were on the watch for each procession as it approached, and it was their
duty to announce the name of the Prince
or Baron as he passed through the gate.

The procession of Baron Ii Kamon-no-
Kami left his mansion at a half past the
5th watch, or 9 A. M. In a few minutes it
came near the Sakurada (Cherry-field) Gate

(one of the inner Mon or fortified entrances
to the Castle and facing south). A few
men dressed like ordinary Samurai with
reddish brown rain-coats, suddenly came
up, and audaciously tried to snatch away
one of the spears. A struggle ensued.
The report of a gun which almost immediately followed, was answered by the
appearance of a band of armed men from
both sides of the street and a bloody fight
at once began.

The guards and retainers of the Baron
were entirely unprepared for this sudden
attack. It was a time when the whole country was in the enjoyment of immemorial
peace. Especially when it rained or snowed,
the sword guards and handles were covered
in a way which made it difficult to un-
sheathe with sufficient readiness. Several

of the Baron's followers, not having time to draw, had to defend themselves with their swords while still in their scabbards. The blows they dealt took effect only when the sheaths, which fortunately were of wood, broke in course of fighting.

This lack of preparation on the part of Naosuké's followers, coupled with covered swords and flowing rain-coats, made it comparatively easy for the assassins to effect their cruel purpose. Still these were not allowed to go unharmed. Two of them were killed on the spot, while three were mortally wounded and fell down on the road. The one who carried off the head of the Baron found himself disabled on account of his wounds, and killed himself at Tatsu-nokuchi, (Dragon's Mouth) a distance of about a mile and a half from the place of

attack. Two others died afterward from
the wounds they had received. The loss
on the part of the Baron's retainers was
four killed, and nineteen wounded, four of
whom afterward died.

The band of assassins consisted of eighteen
men, all of whom were those from the
Mito Clan, except one man who came from
Satsuma. But before they committed their
cruel deed, they had resigned from the clan
to which they belonged, and thus became *rō-
nin* or wave-men. This was in accordance
with feudal tradition, for otherwise they
would have involved their lord in their un-
lawful deed.

Almost in a moment after the report of
the signal gun, Naosuké's kago was surrounded by three or four men with drawn
swords. The guards were overpowered,

and the Baron was stabbed several times through the sides of his palanquin, so that when dragged out he was already dead, yet their vengeance was not yet satisfied, for each dealt a blow at the corpse. It was the Satsuma man who cut off the Baron's head, and started off with it, followed by one of his comrades. The pair were pursued by a retainer of the Baron, Kokawara by name, who although severely wounded yet inspired by devotion to his lord, overtook them and dealt a blow on the head of the Satsuma man. Nevertheless Kokawara was overpowered. The wound he had inflicted had its effect, for it disabled the man from going any farther than Tatsunokuchi, where he hastened death by his own hand.

The whole tragedy was the work of only a few minutes, and when other retainers of

Naosuké prepared to march to the place of attack, it was all over,* and they met the return of their master's kago. Four of the assassins delivered themselves to the Senator Baron Wakizaka, the other four to Baron Hosokawa, while the rest of them made their escape toward Kiôto. They of course deserved capital punishment, and their execution took place in the 7th month of the following year (August 1861).

The name of Hasuła stands first in the principal paper signed by the seventeen assassins in which they stated the reason for their act. The man of Satsuma did not sign the paper although he played so active a part in the cruel deed. There were two

---

* For a full and detailed account, in fiction, but with careful study of the historic background of Ii's assassination, see chapters XXIX—XXXII of Arthur Maclay's, "Mito Yashiki."

papers which they presented to the authorities of the Shōgunate when they delivered
up themselves after their murderous work.
The one was the principal document and
the other was a supplement. The substance
of the principal paper was as follows :—

" While fully aware of the necessity for
some change in policy since the coming of
the Americans to Uraga, it is entirely
against the interest of the country and a
shame to the sacred dignity of the land to
open commercial relations, to admit foreigners into the castle, to conclude a treaty,
to abolish the established custom of tramp-
ling on the picture of Christ, to permit
foreigners to build places of worship of their
evil religion, Christianity, and to allow the
three Ministers to reside in the land. Under
the excuse of keeping the peace, too much

compromise has been made at the sacrifice
of national honor.   Too much fear has been
shown in regard to the foreigners' threatenings.   Not only has the national custom
been set aside, and national dignity injured,
but the policy followed by the Shōgunate
has no Imperial sanction.   For all these
acts the Tairō Baron Ii Kamon-no-Kami is
responsible.

" Taking advantage of the youth of the
Shōgun, he has assumed unbridled power.
In order to effect his own end, his auto-
cracy has gone so far as to confine, under
false charges, the Princes and Barons who
would be faithful and loyal to the cause of
the Imperial Cabinet and of the Shōgunate.
He has proved himself an unpardonable
enemy of this nation.   The power of
government in his hand will be too dan-

gerous for a harmonious relation of the Imperial Cabinet and the Shōgunate, for he has gone so far as to interfere in the matter of the Imperial succession. Our sense of patriotism could not brook this abuse of power at the hands of such a wicked rebel.

"Therefore we have consecrated ourselves to be the instruments of Heaven to punish this wicked man, and we have assumed on ourselves the duty of putting an end to a serious evil by killing this atrocious autocrat. Our conduct, however, does not indicate the slightest enmity to the Shōgunate. We swear before Heaven and earth, gods and men, that our action is entirely built on our hope of seeing the policy of the Shōgunate resume its proper form and abide by the holy and wise will of

His Majesty, the Emperor. We hope to see our national glory manifested in the expulsion of foreigners from the land. Thus will the whole nation be established on a basis as firm and unmoveable as Mount Fuji itself."

Dated, 3rd Month, Seventh year

of Anséi (March, 1850).

Signed by Hasuda and sixteen others.

The supplementary paper was a more minute elucidation of what is stated in the paper just referred to.

Whatever epithets, malice and enmity may have heaped on Naosuké, the mute eloquence of the fruits of his political career now indisputably pleads his merits as a patriot and a statesman of rare ability and of the highest order.

Here, it will be well to remember the

strength of his sense of duty and his con-
tempt of personal safety. This is most
clearly seen in his interview with Baron
Matsudaira of Yada.

Since the time of Prince Rekko's confinement, and especially at the period of
the great agitation in his clan when the
Imperial paper was ordered to be returned,
many feared that attempts might be made
on the life of the Tairō Naosuké.

Baron Matsudaira of Yada, who was an
intimate friend of Naosuké, personally came
to persuade him to resign and thus get
him out of the impending danger.

The Tairō while thanking him for his
kind advice said that his sense of duty
would not allow him to evade his personal
danger in times of great difficulty. " My
own safety is nothing," said he, " when I

see a great danger threatening the future of my country."

His friend then advised him to increase the number of his guards when he went out. Naosuké simply replied that their number being fixed by the statute of the Shōgunate, he as the Tairō, must not form a precedent of freely modifying the established rule for the sake of his personal safety.

Baron Matsudaira became so earnest in his pleading that when Naosuké asked to be excused, as the time came for him to go to the Court, he held the Tairō by one of the sleeves of his dress, urging him to take his advice, and a part of the dress was torn as Naosuké tried to shake off his firm grasp. Seeing that the Tairō's resolve was too strong, the kind Baron before leaving his friend's mansion, told some of Naosuké's retainers to be prepared for an emergency that might be expected at any moment. This was on the 28th day of the 2nd month (March 21st), only a few days before the assassination.

Baron Matsudaira of Yada was not the only person who tried to persuade Naosuké to avoid danger by resigning his office. Several of his own retainers, as well as some of the Shōgun's officers gave him similar advice, but his answer was always the same. " Resignation is easy, but the times are difficult. I will not, and must not, avoid both danger and difficulty on the simple ground of seeking personal ease."

To a person who remarked that his refusal to resign was said to be based on his love of power, he made answer in a poem, a literal translation of which is as follows :

" Spring has not yet advanced to melt the ice on the pure fountain, and none has yet drawn water from its depth."

By the pure fountain he meant his heart, and he regrets that his true intention has not been understood.

Only after many years have his sincerity and true merit come to be seen by the people for whom he had sacrificed his whole being.

"After passing a night of fleeting dreams the flower of the heart opens and blossems to-day" (Katsu).

—FINIS—

www.ingramcontent.com/pod-product-compliance
Lightning Source LLC
Chambersburg PA
CBHW030555040726
47497CB00008B/2733